"*Penelope Wilcock has created a wonderful cast of characters to fill the marvellously accurate fourteenth-century monastery in her medieval series. For the lover of medieval mysteries this is a series not to be missed.*"

Mel Starr, author of *The Chronicles of Hugh de Singleton*

Other titles in the *Hawk and the Dove* series:

The Hawk and the Dove
The Wounds of God
The Long Fall
The Hardest Thing to Do
The Hour Before Dawn
Remember Me
The Breath of Peace
The Beautiful Thread
A Day and a Life (coming June 2016)

The Beautiful Thread

PENELOPE WILCOCK

LION FICTION

Published by Lion Fiction
an imprint of
Lion Hudson plc
Wilkinson House, Jordan Hill Road
Oxford OX2 8DR, England
www.lionhudson.com/fiction

ISBN 978 1 78264 145 2
e-ISBN 978 1 78264 146 9

First edition 2015

Acknowledgments
Scripture quotations marked KJV taken from The Authorized (King
James) Version. Rights in the Authorized Version are vested in the
Crown. Reproduced by permission of the Crown's patentee, Cambridge
University Press.

A catalogue record for this book is available from the British Library

Printed and bound in the UK, January 2016, LH26

This one is

For Rosie, who has a glint of mischief in her eye, even when she is being kind and forbearing.

For Grace, whose undeterred patience, tolerance and compassion is a wonder to us all.

For Hebe, whose soul walks in bare feet, the Earth's friend, wisdom and quietness her native territory.

For Alice, honest, loyal, true; who has the absolute humility of the real artist.

For Fi, who tells me that "No" is not a bad thing to say, and who feels her way to the heart of things.

For Tony, who always looks for the best, and covers my shortcomings with gentleness, goes on believing in me when my hope runs out.

And for Harvey Richardson, who was kind to me.

By this shall all men know that ye are my disciples, if ye have love one to another.
Jesus of Nazareth: John 13:35, KJV

This is my simple religion. There is no need for temples; no need for complicated philosophy. Our own brain, our own heart is our temple; the philosophy is kindness.
The Dalai Lama

Attachment to being right creates suffering. When you have a choice to be right, or to be kind, choose kind and watch your suffering disappear.
Dr Wayne Dyer

There are three ways to ultimate success:
    The first way is to be kind.
    The second way is to be kind.
    The third way is to be kind.
Fred Rogers

Life goes by fast. Enjoy it. Calm down. It's all funny.
Joan Rivers

In your hearts enthrone him; there let him subdue all that is not holy, all that is not true.
Look to him, your Saviour, in temptation's hour; let his will enfold you in its light and power.
Caroline M. Noel

And be ye kind one to another...
Ephesians 4:32, KJV

Contents

The Community of St Alcuin's Abbey   8

Chapter One   11

Chapter Two   43

Chapter Three   73

Chapter Four   106

Chapter Five   140

Chapter Six   174

Glossary and Explanatory Notes   205

Monastic Day   207

Liturgical Calendar   208

The Community of St Alcuin's Abbey

(Not all members are mentioned in *The Beautiful Thread*)

Fully professed monks

Abbot John Hazell	*once the abbey's infirmarian*
Father Francis	*prior*
Brother Cormac	*cellarer*
Father Theodore	*novice master*
Father Gilbert	*precentor*
Father Clement	*overseer of the scriptorium*
Father Dominic	*guest master*
Brother Thomas	*abbot's esquire, also involved with the farm and building repairs*
Father Bernard	*sacristan*
Father Gerard	*almoner*
Brother Martin	*porter*
Brother Thaddeus	*potter*
Brother Michael	*infirmarian*
Brother Damian	*teaches in the school*
Brother Conradus	*kitchener*
Brother Richard	*fraterer*
Brother Stephen	*oversees the abbey farm*
Brother Peter	*ostler*
Brother Josephus	*teaches in the abbey school*
Father James	*makes and mends robes, occasionally works in the scriptorium*
Brother Germanus	*works on the farm, in the wood yard and gardens*
Brother Walafrid	*herbalist, oversees the brew house*
Brother Giles	*assists Brother Walafrid and works in laundry*

Brother Mark	*too old for taxing occupation, but keeps the bees*
Brother Paulinus	*works in the kitchen garden and orchards*
Brother Prudentius	*now old, helps on the farm and in the kitchen garden and orchards*
Brother Fidelis	*now old, oversees the flower gardens*
Brother Basil	*old, assists the sacristan – ringing the bell for the office hours, etc.*

Fully professed monks now confined to the infirmary through frailty of old age

Father Gerald	*once sacristan*
Brother Denis	*once a scribe*
Father Paul	*once precentor*
Brother Edward	*onetime infirmarian, now living in the infirmary but active enough to help there and occasionally attend Chapter and the daytime hours of worship*

Novices

Brother Benedict	*main assistant in the infirmary*
Brother Boniface	*helps in the scriptorium*
Brother Cassian	*works in the school*
Brother Cedd	*helps in the scriptorium and when required in the robing room*
Brother Felix	*helps Father Gilbert*
Brother Placidus	*helps on the farm*
Brother Robert	*assists in the pottery*

Members of the community mentioned in earlier stories and now deceased

Abbot Gregory of the Resurrection

Abbot Columba du Fayel (also known as Father Peregrine)

| Father Matthew | *novice master* |
| Brother Andrew | *kitchener* |

Brother Cyprian	*porter*
Father Aelred	*schoolmaster*
Father Lucanus	*novice master before Father Matthew*
Father Anselm	*once robe-maker*

Chapter One

William stared uncomprehending at the ceiling. Bewildered, he half raised himself on his elbows and turned his head towards the window where the early sun flooded through in such glory this May morning that it had awoken him. He sat up completely, in consternation now, his heart racing. This was not his cell. Moments ago he had been immersed in an exceedingly pleasant dream enjoying an interlude of sublimely conjugal sweetness with Madeleine, and now... This was not his cottage, either. For one fleeting instant he wondered if he was going mad, if he had dreamed his entire marriage; then he remembered where he was. Relief flooded over him. St Alcuin's guesthouse. He had come to help Cormac with the complications that had arisen from the bishop's visit coinciding with this infernal wedding.

Allowing himself to sink back, trembling, onto his uncompromising monastic pillow, he wondered bitterly why he seemed to have been doomed to spend his entire life in a perpetual panic.

He let no more than a few moments pass. Self-pity feeds on itself and is futile. He kicked the blanket off and swung his legs over the edge of the low bedframe.

Unsure of the time, he padded downstairs to the garderobe and lavatorium. Nobody about. They must be in chapel, then. Often the guestmaster would stay at his post, but William

11

guessed Brother Dominic must be taking advantage of the days remaining before visitors began to trickle in for the wedding. And the bishop. Best not forget him. But for the moment, Dominic probably judged William knew his way round well enough, and had gone to chapel. Putting his head round the refectory door, he saw a pewter plate set out on the table, a basket of bread rolls, a covered dish presumably containing butter, a flagon of ale, a beaker, a napkin. They'd not forgotten him, then.

As he loped up the stairs again to dress properly, he heard the Mass bell begin tolling, which let him know the time of day. He wondered what to do about that. Abbot John had in private given him Eucharist, but in the community setting he was as good as excommunicated, having broken his vows and walked out on them to marry Madeleine. Such things were not – ever – outlived. Best leave them to it and stick with Vespers and Compline. Or maybe go to the parish Mass later on, let folk assume he'd made his communion elsewhere earlier. Or...

Then, impatient at the uneasiness of it all, he shrugged the deliberations away and came out into the daylight. Now would be as good a time as any to prowl quietly round the kitchens, the stores, the stables, the scriptorium – take a look at the level of provision, judge if things looked healthy and well in hand. He wanted to see the infirmary (but that would not be unattended) and the sacristy (but that meant passing through the church within possible sight of the choir). Obviously he wanted to cast an eye over the books in the checker, but that would be locked. At least, he assumed Brother Cormac locked up when he left it empty. There was too much money and information in there not to turn a key against prying eyes and pilfering fingers. Brother Cormac... Abbot John had appointed him to the obedience of cellarer at William's recommendation. Was it turning out well? He dearly hoped so.

An hour later, having entered and inspected every storehouse and place of work he thought might be available and empty, satisfied that all seemed in good order, William made his way to the abbot's house. Though his quiet, thorough searches had taken him into the cloister, he walked round to the door in the front range. Here in the abbey court guests would congregate. Across the greensward here they approached the church through its great west door. This door to the abbot's house was a public entrance, for visitors. The cloister door was for the community; and William no longer had a right to that entrance.

Knocking and, as expected, finding no answer – they would be in Chapter now – William tried the latch and found the door unbolted. This was a trusting place. And maybe kindness earned the freedom to trust. The village loved its abbey, and all who knew them held these brothers in high esteem. They were good men. It was like John to leave his door open for anyone who wanted to come in.

William stood quite still in the abbot's atelier, breathing the familiar scents of woodsmoke, beeswax, stone, herbs. He felt the movement of love in the private depths of his heart, for this man and this place; this community.

He sat down quietly on one of the two chairs close to the swept hearth. Sunlight diffused softly through the small windows. He watched motes of dust drift, catching the brightness of its rays. He allowed memories of this room in the abbot's house to emerge and float up inside him, some of healing, some of harsh agony. All of them of formation and transformation, the making of his soul. Without moving he let the ghosts of the past parade. He had no regret for his place here, but the bonds of affection... no; deeper than that – belonging, love... their roots grew into the living tissue of his being... or into the stonework of this house of prayer... depending how you looked at it...

The sharp click of the latch to the cloister door curtailed his musing. He looked up, and rose to his feet as Brother Tom the abbot's esquire came into the room.

13

"I hope I'm not presumptuous, barging in like this –" he began, but got no further, finding himself wrapped in Tom's hearty embrace of welcome: "Eh, but it's grand to have thee back!"

And then Abbot John was with them: "God love you, it's so good to see you, William! So kind of you to come. Man, but it brings my heart joy to see the glare of those baleful eyes once again! Did you sleep well? Have you breakfasted? No? But they put something out for you? We haven't left you to starve? When did you get in – last night? I looked for you at Compline. Brother Thomas – if it's not too much trouble, would you fetch over some bread and cheese and ale for William to break his fast here – I'm getting somewhat of a sense of urgency about the tasks before us and we have much to discuss. Thank you, Brother, thank you. Now then – let's bring your chair to my table here. That's right. So. You'll be pleased with me – I've a sheaf of lists and plans to keep us enthralled through the morning. What d'you want to talk about first? Cormac's progress? The wedding? The bishop? Or have you news of your own? All is well with you and Madeleine?"

William sat down in his chair, the baleful eyes regarding his brother-in-law with a glow of pure happiness. It felt good to be back.

"I've given the place a quick once-over while you were in chapel," he said. "Bishops and their Visitations are a familiar hell. So tell me about the wedding."

"Very well, then. Let me relate but a little and you will quickly grasp – this is set fair to be the wedding of the century. Not like yours – a man, his wife and a witness. Oh no. We are expecting upwards of a hundred and fifty guests, despite my striving to keep the numbers down. A party of minstrels has been ordered – with jugglers, so I'm promised. We have a harpist coming, and talk of flutes, lutes, drums and horns. I've said an absolute no to wrestling but yes to skittles. And no to apple-bobbing because

14

what apples we have left we shall need to raid impressively to feed them all.

"The banns are read, no objections. Unless you count the profound opposition of the bridegroom's mother."

"Who is – ?"

"Nobody in particular – it's not so much who she is as what she thinks she is – and the lip-curling lack of esteem with which she regards poor Hannah. Not that she need think we'd be putting ourselves out for them to this extent if Hannah were not Brother Damian's sister.

"Damian's father is a freeman, has about fourteen acres of his own land – put to barley, oats, peas, a few sheep and his house cows. The usual chickens and a pig of course; and then you've maybe seen Hannah out and about with her goats on the moor. She takes them to browse. Her family are good people. Cheerful, intelligent, kind. Hannah's mother Margery's a sensible woman, and her father works hard. There's another lad – Peter – and the father's Walter. Walter Mitchell. Honest, capable, pretty much what you'd expect if you know Brother Damian.

"But the lad Hannah's set her heart on – Gervase Bonvallet – is born of a tribe with rather more airs and graces. Florence is his mother, comes with a *very* keen sense of her place in the world. Father is Cecil, and Gervase has two brothers, Hubert and Percival. The Bonvallets are farmers, same as the Mitchells, but the difference is that Cecil has a knighthood, two hundred acres, and plenty in store.

"The way Florence sees it, Hannah would do very well as a serving wench, but she's no choice at all for a Bonvallet bride. A comely enough lass in a common way, but decidedly too rustic for Florence's tastes. We've been all through it. Florence has argued and protested, stormed and pleaded, said this marriage has ruined her life's work and will take her down to an early grave. She has no quarrel with Hannah as... er... a playmate for young Gervase;

Hannah's clean of lice and diseases, she's a fresh and pleasant, sweet-natured girl. It's just that Florence can't envisage her as a Bonvallet. She imagined an altogether more delicate and gently born helpmeet when it comes to the family name."

William listened to this with interest and amusement. "I see," he said. "And what about the menfolk? Sir Cecil? Walter? They like each other? Or do they oppose the match?"

John shrugged. "Up here in the hills – well, who is there? Sir Cecil has his head screwed on. Walter's a good farmer, and an honest man. Hannah may not be an aspirational catch, but her family will bring no shame or trouble. They aren't brawlers or drinkers. They do well with what they have. In this decade of wet summers when food has been so scarce, Walter's had meat salted away, grain in store, dried fruits aplenty. He's got through where others have starved – and helped his neighbours too. He's a shrewd man. And Sir Cecil's no fool; he respects ability.

"The lads of both families all grew up together of course, they're good friends. Margery is proud as punch, thinks Hannah has an excellent catch in Gervase – as so she does. It's only Florence; but when I say 'only'... Well, Florence... still, you'll meet her maybe."

"And the wedding is in a fortnight's time, you tell me?"

"It is."

"All provisions in? Well prepared? Ready for the onslaught?"

John hesitated, evidently unsure.

"Well... we are; yes, we *are*. Thanks to the legacy from Mother Cottingham, we've been comfortably off this last year. We took heed of all you told us we lacked, and have set about stocking up with everything needed to bump up our earnings. Even in times when others are struggling under money troubles and failed harvests, we seem to be getting through without feeling the pinch too badly."

"Besides," William interrupted him, "it's presumably not you who will be paying for this wedding? John? Whatever of your comestibles may be sequestered for the feast, Sir Cecil will surely make good? Cormac is keeping careful tally? Reassure me!"

"Oh, aye." John waved his hand vaguely. "We'll keep account. We'll get it back, I've no doubt. And if we didn't it wouldn't be the end of the world."

William shook his head at this casual attitude, then addressed the hesitancy he had detected in John's tone. "But?" He looked at the abbot enquiringly. "What's the 'but'? I can hear it in your voice."

"Oh – it's a question of finding enough hands for all the preparations. Brother Conradus is a wonder, and we have the lads from the village helping in the kitchen, as well as Brother Damian when he can be spared from the school – I moved him there from the infirmary, and he's doing well. But every man here has his work to do, and I can't see how we can release many of them for cooking. Besides which, even if we did, the sort of delicacies Brother Conradus has in mind will be beyond the abilities of Thaddeus or Germanus or Richard, even supposing they had time on their hands. Brother Conradus looks worried – which isn't like him; he's usually equal to anything culinary we ask of him. I'm not sure just exactly what we're going to do. I thought of asking Madeleine to come and help, but I know how it is; you have fowls and beasts of your own, and soft fruit coming on. I don't see how your place could do without the both of you."

William frowned thoughtfully, turning the matter over in his mind. John was right. Their homestead could not possibly be left unattended.

A knock interrupted them. Brother Tom set down the tray of food he'd just brought in, and turned back to answer the cloister door.

"Ah! Brother Conradus!" The abbot half rose from his chair. "Come in – we were just talking about making ready for the wedding. William is here, as you see – come to give Brother Cormac a hand in the checker, juggling the bishop's visit with Hannah's marriage. I was only explaining this minute that though we have the provisions we're woefully shorthanded. Have you a moment to tell him something of what you propose? Is it all carried about in your head or written down somewhere? I have the lists you gave me along with all the others here, if your memory needs a jog."

William formed an impression of something in full sail as the young kitchener approached them. A few months of overseeing the abbey's culinary provision had impressively augmented his girth. But more than this, the kindness, the enthusiasm in his smiling face billowed about him and shone ahead of him, like gulls and bright sunshine around a small ship making good headway on a fair, breezy day.

"Father William!" he exclaimed. "Good morrow! Ah, how splendid to see you!"

In the last hour William thought he'd been met by a more loving and magnificently hospitable welcome than in all of his life before. He noted the sense of happiness cautiously establishing in his core.

Brother Conradus began eagerly to outline the complexities and challenges of preparing his feast, while simultaneously keeping the brethren and their steep accumulation of overnight guests well fed. His exact and detailed knowledge of every morsel they had in store and on order became impressively clear as he talked. He knew the capacity of their milk cows and the laying averages of their hens. He knew how much of what they had could be used and how much should be kept back to see the community onward. He had calculated their likely harvest produce (if they were spared deluging rain this time, but also if they were not), and assessed how low they could therefore run down what they had put by. William listened to him with evident approval, pleased to see the ambitious project ahead in such competent hands, as Conradus waved the list about, not needing to consult it to explain its many implications.

"It's a joy – it's all a joy, of course," said the kitchener. "I'm tremendously looking forward to it. I'm just not quite sure how… well… there's only one of me and nobody else quite up to – at least, of course… umm… The subtleties are what I'm really worried about."

William nodded thoughtfully. He could see that.

"There must be three at least, possibly four if we have soup as well."

"Four what?" John frowned, puzzled.

"Four subtleties." Conradus looked at his abbot in helpful clarification, but quickly saw he'd drawn a blank. "There has to be a subtlety after every course," he explained.

William grinned at John's complete incomprehension. Raised by a wise-woman herbalist on the outskirts of a hamlet high in the hills at Motherwell, exchanging the moors and the woodland streams for a life of work and prayer in St Alcuin's infirmary, John hadn't even a nodding acquaintance with lavish and elaborate formal feasts.

"Oh!" The young monk flushed, perceiving his abbot to be at a loss and ashamed at having set his superior at a disadvantage. "Forgive me, Father – I should have expressed myself more clearly. So thoughtless. I was all trammelled with my own cares and preoccupations – like St Martha – I'm so sorry. I've been too wrapped up in myself."

"Not to worry," said his abbot. "So… ?"

"Oh! Well, a subtlety is the fantastical centrepiece that crowns each course. Something in pastry usually – though I'd thought I could make a dragon out of artfully arranged shortbreads, with a marzipan head and maybe spun sugar wings, for the sweet course." Conradus gesticulated excitedly as he spoke, then caught himself.

He paused in recollection of appropriate humility. "That is – if I may have permission to get the sugar, of course. If the expense is not too great. Lady Florence said I shouldn't cut corners, and I thought... well, a dragon would be easy.

"But the others should speak something of the occasion – a representation of the bride and the groom – but also of the holy solemnity. I ought to attempt a Holy Trinity in pastry, or a gingerbread monastery with gilded crenellations perhaps. I thought I could make a whole community and a bride and groom in bread dough, and a chalice and paten on an altar, egg-washed to make them shine. I haven't really finished thinking it through, to be honest; because every time I hit the obstacle of shortage of time. I know the obstacle is the path, Father, and we should make light of adversity under every circumstance, and I do my best, truly. But even with the right attitude, time is pressing."

Abbot John listened to him, trying to keep from his expression any trace of the incredulity he privately felt. "Subtlety" seemed the right word; and irrelevance, superfluity, inanity or extravagance would have done right well as an alternative. However he could have got his community mixed up in all this, with the bishop's Visitation looming on the horizon, he could hardly begin to imagine.

Then, "Why don't we send for your mother?" asked William. "She is but twenty miles away, is she not? Would she come? If someone rides today, we could have her back here in three days."

The young man stopped short, his gaze arrested at William, his mouth dropped slightly ajar, his eyes shining. "What a wonderful, brilliant idea!" he exclaimed. "Oh, I wonder if she could."

John now found himself fixed by the enquiring gaze of two pairs of eyes: one cool, amused, the colour of the sea, one brown and shining as new conkers.

"For sure," he said. "That should get us out of a hole. Write her a note and some directions to your family's home. I'll send Father Chad."

"Shall I go and tell him?" offered Brother Tom; and within the hour the matter was settled. Armed with a letter from Conradus, with a postscript from the abbot and closed with his seal, and a carefully drawn map of where to find the homestead, Father Chad saddled up and set off in search of Brother Conradus's mother. She had by this time become established as a legend at St Alcuin's, so much had they heard from Conradus of her guiding wisdom and gentle counsel. If Brother Conradus's mother was on her way, things would be all right.

"William, that was an excellent suggestion. Remind me of her name, Brother," said Abbot John.

"Rose." Conradus spoke softly, his voice full of affection and pride. "My mother is called Rose."

His abbot smiled. "A lovely name," he said. "Like a summer's day. I look forward to meeting her." For a moment the thoughts conjured up by her name distracted him. Fragrant blossom. Blue skies. Honey bees. Warm afternoons drifting gently into the peace of evening. A world away from endless administration and the management of difficult people. Rose. So pretty.

"Ah," said Conradus, earnest and happy, "you will love her, Father John. You will absolutely love her. Everyone loves my mother. She has the gift."

Looking at Brother Conradus, John thought that was probably true. Certainly she'd done a good job raising her son, he thought, as he watched that young man heading back to the kitchen fifteen minutes later, excited and happy at the prospect of his mother – so dearly beloved – being on hand to help him.

But for now the abbot had to put his mind to Lady Florence Bonvallet. "Will you join us, William?" he asked. "I know you have matters in hand with Brother Cormac; but I'd like you to meet her. How can we work that, I wonder?"

William shrugged. "Tell her you've engaged me as the steward for the feast."

"Oh – yes, that would suffice. She will be coming to see me later on this morning. Can I send to the checker for you, when she arrives?"

"You may indeed. But will you show me your own inventories before I go, so I have clear in my mind what's expected specifically for the wedding?" He reached out for the sheaf of lists John passed him across the table. "Thank you," he said, scanning the contents with interest. Without pausing in his perusal he added, "And tell me a bit about the bishop's visit before I get going. I can listen and read at the same time. He is coming when?"

"He's due in four days' time, and – God willing – his stay will in no way overlap with the Bonvallet wedding. He should take maybe three days to look over everything and ask anything he wishes. Then on his way, and we're done for another year, with a week in hand to get everything ready for the wedding."

"Bishop Eric, isn't it? I know him well enough, of course, but how do you find him as a Visitor? Picky, I should imagine, and demanding. Not easy."

The abbot shifted uneasily in his chair. He did not like Bishop Eric, but to say so would be disloyal and arrogant. He hesitated.

"Oh dear," said William, without looking up.

"No, no! All will be well, I have no doubt. He... Bishop Eric – well, you know him – he has very traditional views. He can be insistent on points of church law – likes to make sure we follow to a nicety all that the Rule lays upon us; as so we should. He... well, he can seem inflexible at times, but... on the other hand, it's always possible to jolly him up with something tasty to eat, because he does like his food. He can be searching in his enquiries about our fiscal arrangements."

"In what sense?" William glanced up momentarily. "You mean he'll be sniffing around to see if there's any money to be had? Yes? Ah, then in heaven's name do yourself a favour, John, and brush across the tracks of Ellen Cottingham's massive legacy. You had an elderly widow leave some money to the abbey, but times are hard; you had big losses – a ship lost at sea, harvests failing year after year in the rains. It's cost you dear, you've about scraped through, but –"

John interrupted him, laughing. "I get the picture! Yes, surely, I'll do what I can."

William nodded, satisfied, laying down the inventory of pewter-ware and spoons on his pile of checked lists, as he looked at Brother Thaddeus's rough jottings from the pottery, indicating what would go into the next firing. It was hard to decipher this. Some of the numbers were back to front, he wrote every "d" as a "b", and much of what he'd set down had been obscured by spatters and smears of clay slip. William peered at it, adjusting the angle he held it to catch the light.

"And his staff? Who's he got for his equerry – that's who will be his main go-between with Brother Cormac. Anyone I know?"

Abbot John picked up his stylus and tablet from the tabletop in front of him, and fiddled with them. "Brainard LePrique," he said. At that, William raised his eyes from the stack of parchments.

"What? Who did you say? Brainard LePrique?"

The abbot refused to be drawn by his incredulous grin. He said only, "I think it sounds better with a French accent."

"Oh! I beg his pardon! *Brrrain-arrrr*? Is that better?"

John would not rise to this. "They did not elect me abbot to mock my guests," he said simply. William just looked at him. Thirty years in a monastery had taught him the habit of saying everything while saying nothing. "Well? Do you know him?" John asked.

"No, *mon Père*. I have never had the pleasure of making the acquaintance of *Brainard LePrique*. But I certainly know Bishop Eric. Self-righteous, cruel, greedy, unforgiving, and does not like me one tiny little bit."

"It would seem that's mutual," said John. "You do have a remarkable gift for making friends."

William shrugged. "It's been said. But not by many." He flicked the parchment in his left hand with the fingers of his right. "Well, this lot's looking… terrifying. I see why you sent for me. Who's been helping Brother Cormac in the checker up until now? By my soul, these nuptials are going to rack up a prodigious bill." He began to tot up Brother Conradus's careful itemization. "It comes to…"

"It seemed to me," said the abbot, "that the man best placed to understand what Cormac needs to know is Father Chad. He's so long been our prior. Francis is new in that obedience; he's having to learn as fast as Cormac is. So I asked Chad to advise him a bit."

William didn't look up. "Oh, yes – Father Chad," he murmured, running his finger down the column of figures, calculating as he went: "taking mediocrity to the next level. What would you do without him?"

He continued to peruse the document until he was no longer able to ignore John's silence. He let his hand rest on the parchment, quite still, and raised his eyes from the tidy lines of figures.

"I'm sorry," he said quietly. "That wasn't kind, was it? To sneer at a man who is doing the best he can. Of your charity, will you overlook that? It reflects badly on me, not on him. This is why I have my gift for making friends you mentioned. I'm sorry, John. Anyway –" He got to his feet. "This all makes sense and I have it in mind now. If that's everything for the moment, I'll head on over to the checker; see if your cellarer has the same tight grasp on all the goings-on as your kitchener." He paused. "Am I forgiven?"

"For your caustic and merciless contempt of your fellow man? Yes, I should think so."

"Thank you." William offered the abbot a small ceremonial bow.

As the door closed behind him, Abbot John wondered if perhaps he had worried unnecessarily about the days ahead. With such competent, able men under his roof, maybe everything would roll smoothly. In three weeks' time he might be looking back wondering why he'd felt so apprehensive. He said as much to Brother Tom. "And it's good to see William again," he added. "He brings a certain something that no one else does!"

"Oh, yes," said Tom. "Makes my heart glad to see that familiar scowl about the place again – finding fault with everything and keeping us all on our toes."

✠   ✠   ✠

Pleased to find Brother Cormac alone in the checker, William asked to see the ledgers, any orders or unpaid bills, along with any lists from the guesthouse to help get a grip on numbers and timing for the hospitality required of them in the next few weeks.

"It's not only the details you have to get right," he commented, looking swiftly – but thoroughly – through the stack of parchments Cormac thumped onto the table in front of him: "it's the principles. Attitudes of mind. Anticipation – you have to see what's coming before it gets here. This isn't Cana in Galilee. We'll have to be sure we do actually have enough wine in the cellar. Flexibility – you must be ready to move men, money, stores to cover whatever's needed, plug gaps. To do that, to respond quickly and appropriately, keep everything running smoothly, you have to know exactly what's available to you. What's in store, what's coming in, where to put it all with everything accessible and in the right order, oldest stuff closest to hand. And of course you have to bear in mind any regular outgoings that may alter what you can count on. It has to be all there in your imagination, like a landscape continually before your inner eye, everything charted and repeatedly checked."

Intent on his explanation, simultaneously examining the stacks of reminders, lists, notes and bills, he glanced quickly at Cormac for his response, then relaxed into a grin.

"I'll help you," he reassured him. "It's mostly about application and familiarity. You have to know it and care about it. It's the body of the abbey, this obedience. The abbot looks after its soul and the prior should be its mind – noticing, remembering – but you care for its body. Just as if you have a horse, you must make sure it's not too hot or cold, has been fed enough of the right things at the right time but not too much, that it's exercised, groomed, has somewhere to shelter, is properly shod, dosed when need be, mucked out. The list is long, true enough, but second nature for anyone who knows horses. This abbey is the same, like a living thing you're caring for. There's nothing static about it, it's dynamic, nothing ever stays the same for two hours together. You have to be paying attention and alert to the consequences implicit in every change."

Cormac looked overwhelmed.

"This is the importance of meticulous record-keeping and faithful checking. It's not easy, but it isn't hard either, if you see what I mean. It just has to be done."

Both men looked up as a shadow in the doorway heralded the approach of a stranger. The checker stood alone in the abbey court, between the gatehouse and the west range of the main buildings. The door stood open when warm weather permitted, and after the porter's lodge and the guesthouse, this was where any visitors at a loss or with an enquiry often called. All tradesmen brought their bills of work and were paid off here. The two men took in the twinkling eyes and curving lips, the expensively attired figure, of a man neither of them recognized.

"Can I help you?" Brother Cormac rose to his feet.

"Ah! It's a beautiful day in a beautiful world," announced the newcomer. "Everyday blessings keep us smiling! His Lordship sends warmest kindly greetings, and wants to let you know we made good time so we're here a day earlier than expected. Our smiles have travelled the miles to share in great fellowship with you, and we trust we won't be putting you to any inconvenience."

"Er... what? His Lordship? You're saying... the bishop is here already? He's arrived?"

"Yes, his Lordship is waiting at the guesthouse. I've been looking for your abbot but found only his esquire – so I came here. Our horses will need watering, and his Lordship will be pleased with a hearty repast – we've been on the road three hours."

Cormac felt, beneath the cover of the table behind which he stood, the meaningful pressure of his companion's boot against his ankle. Press, press, press. Why? He realized that his response must sound distinctly lukewarm in respect of its hospitality.

"I'll... um... I'll be right over," he said hastily. "If you'll make yourselves comfortable, I'll just dash down to the kitchen and see what... I'll be right there. Is there anything else I can do for you meanwhile?"

The man cocked his head, bright eyes sparkling. "Smile!" he reprimanded. His own smile remained fixedly in place, encouraging emulation. Cormac stared at him, bewildered.

"Who... who are you?" he asked. The visitor threw back his head and laughed.

"I am Brainard LePrique!"

If Cormac had not felt so taken aback, he might well have laughed at that himself; but as things were, the information just made everything feel even more bizarre.

"His Lordship's equerry?" prompted the enquirer, his head at so sharp an angle now and his eyebrows raised so high that he looked definitely peculiar.

"Oh. I see. Er... welcome. You are welcome indeed. Right then, I'll cut along to the kitchen directly."

The equerry gave a blithe little chuckle, and turned on his heel. "We'll expect you very soon," he said. "His Lordship enjoys paté and red wine, but does not care for pickles. He likes plenty of butter and will never say no to cold cuts of pigeon or guinea-fowl – even peacock if you have it. Lark's tongue paté is his favourite. Or the livers. Oh! Cheer up, Brother! Remember – a smile is the candle in your window that lets the world know a caring, sharing man is there within!"

He headed off with no further remarks. Stupefied, Brother Cormac stared after him, then said to his silent companion. "What the –?"

"A well-fed snake, if I'm not mistaken," responded William tersely. "Expect trouble and keep him where you can see him."

Like a man in a dream, Cormac turned to look at him after a moment's silence. "William," he said, "I – I – I can't do that. I can't."

William frowned, perplexed, then his face cleared. "Oh. Eating skylarks. No. Good for you! Look, all he means is dainties. Cormac, Brother Conradus is your secret weapon here. Tell him to slather on the butter and gild the gingerbread. What that man wants is power, that's all. He's just letting you know how important he is. Play up to it, and quietly forget about the larks. Oh, and Brother Cormac – it would seem this is your chance to unleash the magic of your smile. Or just throw up. Your choice."

Before Cormac could reply to this, a footfall outside and a tap on the door claimed their attention; the porter, Brother Martin.

"Pardon if I'm intruding when you're busy. I've just come from the abbot's house. Lady Florence is here, and Father John asked would I let William know. He says, sorry to trouble you but he'll be glad if you can go over directly."

"Thanks, Brother Martin; I'm on my way. Have you told him Bishop Eric's arrived? Yes? Good. And that's all in hand, is it? The

28

guesthouse, the kitchen – everyone aware? Yes? My word, this place runs like an oiled wheel these days!"

William set out briskly across the broad, open space of the abbey court, enjoying the fragrance of the flowers now blooming in its borders – gillyflowers and violets, some late primroses, cowslips and irises, hellebores, lungwort and lily of the valley. Rosemary bushes in first flower, new green growth of lavender thrusting out from the silver foliage left from last year. And sprays of roses fastened back against the walls, their young leaves shiny copper red, and the buds still small. Such life here, he thought; such happiness.

Brother Thomas opened the door to his knock at the abbot's house, and William stepped in to be introduced as steward of the feast, to Lady Florence Bonvallet and an upright, aged dame occupying the other chair – "Lady Gunhilde Neville – Lady Florence's mother."

"My lady… my lady…" William bowed low, did not attempt to kiss the hand of either, his declared role being too subordinate for such intimacy.

"The steward of the feast," observed Lady Florence, her eye resting appraisingly on William. "So it's too late. It's really happening, and there's nothing more that can be done to stop it."

John invited William to sit with a friendly gesture, and they both sat on stools since the ladies had the chairs.

"Too late?" the abbot enquired cautiously.

"Oh! Maybe you don't think so?" A shaft of hope gleamed in Lady Florence's penetrating eye. "Well, at least I can console myself I've done what I can. I had a most stormy interview with Gervase last week. I thought I was being fair to the girl. I even offered for us to take on the children – save her the expense of their upbringing. I expect we could find a place for them, and a suitable occupation."

"The children?" Abbot John frowned, perplexed. "*Hannah's* children? An occupation? One's barely three and the other but a babe."

"Yes, yes, I know. Well I expect they could be accommodated out of the way somewhere."

"But... why...?"

"Presumably" – Lady Florence fixed the abbot coldly with her gaze and explained with exaggerated clarity – "what she wants is money. And the children will be an impediment if this match does not go ahead. So I offered to step in. If that's what it takes to get rid of her, we can take the children so she is free of that burden, and even give her some small settlement in consideration of the time and expense involved in rearing them thus far. I am sensible of our obligations. I suppose they must *be* Gervase's."

John blinked.

"In my day," interposed the lady's ancient mother, her eyes glittering like jewels of Whitby jet set into a lacy skein of wrinkles, "such audacity would have been unthinkable. Even the most froward upstart would have stopped short of thinking herself capable of worming a way into the Neville family. Or the Bonvallets. Nobody in my generation would have contemplated anything of the sort. Young people nowadays seem to think family doesn't matter – it's all about love. Love! Ha! What do they know? Abandoning all standards, all sense of decency."

She drew back slightly in her chair, her face giving the impression of having detected an offensive odour in the near vicinity. Whether the abbot replied or not seemed a matter of complete indifference to her.

"Gervase said he would have none of it," Lady Florence continued. "He spoke to me most pugnaciously – with extreme disrespect. He insists on seeing this whim through. But what will he do with her once he's got her? Does he imagine he can bring her home? To our manor? She is coarse – common in the extreme. She is of most inferior stuff. She has a certain competence in practical matters, I suppose. I gather she tends a flock of goats out on the moors. But her accomplishments and abilities are those of the lower orders. Gervase brought her once to our house – it was an absolute disaster. They had a fair on the green that day, and he'd promised to take her. She wanted to see the man with the hurdy-gurdy, she said, and the children dancing." (Lady Gunhilde's lip curled as she heard this, and she turned aside her head in incredulous disdain.) "But Gervase and his brothers – Hubert and Percival; I think you know them – wanted to practise their bowmanship, out upon the lawns. Her duty of course was to encourage and admire, but after only a couple of hours she became positively petulant. She wandered away eventually, and Gervase had to stop what he was doing and go in search of her. He found her curled up like a child on a garden bench, *weeping*. Can you imagine? All because she'd missed the fair! That's the kind of girl she is, you see: childish. She can't help it; it's just that she's from that kind of family. Preoccupied with trinkets and baubles, with diversions and amusements. She has no backbone, she doesn't know her duty – she has no idea how to behave."

"It wouldn't have been like that in my day," Lady Gunhilde observed. "*We* knew how to behave. My generation had the highest standards instilled into us. Young people today think any slipshod nonsense will do. I expect it's the way I grew up, but my generation had values. We knew what was expected of us."

"So I felt there was no more I could do," Lady Florence concluded. "I told Gervase it was still not too late to bring things to a halt. But he refused even to answer me – he turned away with extreme discourtesy. I shall entreat him one last time, on the night before his wedding – because I cannot believe he really wants to marry this wench. It can come to no good. What can he possibly see in her, after all?"

Bleak and arid, her coldly questioning eye directed its glance at the abbot. Evidently this was the moment for his response.

William raised his head and looked at John, at the ladies, impassively observing. John sat thinking, rubbed his chin, his mouth.

"I regard this as a very poor return on all we have invested in him," added Lady Florence, seeing the abbot not about to speak. "I don't know how much your father put into your education, Father John – into the moulding of you to become a man fit to enter society – but you will realize it is a costly endeavour, in terms of effort, time and money. One needs a proper foundation to know how to comport oneself with refinement and dignity. It doesn't just come naturally. It is very disappointing to see it thrown away like this. Very disappointing indeed. Gervase has wasted the family resources. One could call it theft, without overstating the matter."

"My lady," asked William quietly and smoothly into the silence that followed this; "are you intimating that the planned marriage may actually not take place?"

"Not if I can help it." Lady Florence sounded not so much vehement as resigned. "But it seems my counsel is not wanted. A mother is not to be consulted. So far as I know it will go ahead. But not by my wish."

"When I grew up," added her mother, "young people respected their parents: 'Honour thy father and thy mother that it may go well with thee, and thou mayest dwell long in the land.' What happened to that? Young people today are grown so headstrong – they think of nothing but pleasing themselves and going their own way. My generation would never have dreamed of such a thing. But I suppose it must have been the way I grew up."

"Yes, my lady," murmured William in the familiar dulcet tone that filled John with immediate alarm, "I suppose it must have been."

Lady Florence's calm, implacable gaze continued to rest on the abbot.

"I know what you are thinking, Father John," she said. That recalled his attention from William.

Few things irritated John more than people telling him they knew what he was thinking. Knowing his annoyance likely to show, however hard he tried to hide it, he lowered his eyes. Flashing unbidden into his mind, a memory of his father surprised him. From his childhood, when Jude had been briefly at home between military skirmishes. They had stood outside in the breezy air, Jude showing his small son how to handle a longbow.

Beautiful yew wood, John could still remember the feel of the thing, ludicrously big for him. His father's touch light upon him – his back, his shoulders, his arms. The kindly voice explaining, "It's not the strength of your arms, lad, you press your whole body into it. Rest your hand so – that's it – and lay your body into the thing. Steady. Hold steady. Hold the strength of your core. Feel it in your belly. That's it, lad." His father's smile. "That's it, lad."

And John, holding steady, raised his eyes to her ladyship, feeling more than seeing William's quick, perceptive, appraising glance checking that all was well.

"You are thinking," said Lady Florence, "that I am a heartless and selfish woman; but you are wrong. Why should I care what happens to Hannah? I have nothing against her – except that she means to ruin the life of my son. I am a mother, and it is in the nature of things that a mother will fight for her child's wellbeing. I do not want that… chit… to exploit my son's vulnerability as a man to press her own advantage. I would spare him the pain such an alliance must bring him in the end, when lust is spent and she and he tire of each other. I would save my son."

John's hand moved in a gesture of involuntary protest. "I do see – but my lady, is that really what's happening? I have met

33

with Gervase and Hannah, counselled them, heard then, listened carefully to what they have to say. Their betrothal has been long – heavens, they have two children already – and the love between them seems real and abiding, to me. The Mitchells are not the Nevilles nor the Bonvallets, I grant you, but they are worthy people. Walter Mitchell is a fine and honourable man. Hannah is the soul of kindness – not gently born maybe, not always dignified – but surely she could learn from you? She is a good mother and she would be a good wife. She has been steadfast in her affections for Gervase these three or four years; Hannah is nothing to be ashamed of."

Lady Florence's lips curved faintly in a small, dismissive smile. Her gaze beheld the abbot in cool pity. "Father John," she said, "how can I put it to you? You are the abbot of a monastery. Whatever your own background, you must surely see the rectitude of precedence, of keeping to the place to which one is assigned. In your abbey, when you enter the room, the brothers rise to their feet. When you reprimand them, they kiss the floor. When you bid them, they go. That's how it is. They do not command you, but you them. This is not because of any tie of personal affection, nor does it imply they have a slavish disposition. It is simply that they know their place and keep to it – and that is what divine order *is*. Knowing and fulfilling our position in life. You are the abbot of St Alcuin's. I am the wife of Sir Cecil Bonvallet and the daughter of Sir Arthur Nevill. I am the mother of my three sons. My role in life is to uphold the wellbeing of my family and to advance its interests as best I may, just as yours is to safeguard the integrity of the Benedictine life in this community. Hannah is nothing to me. I bear her no personal animosity. But she is not of our kind. She does not belong in my family. And if I can get rid of her, I will. But I perceive you to be intractable in your adherence to the point of view Gervase thinks he has. I would request only that you ask yourself, whose side are you on?"

"Whose *side*? Lady Florence, is that what it must come to? I thought this was a marriage, a union – a family – not a war! I'm not on your side or Hannah's side – I see no sides, no opposition. I am on the side of Christ, of love, of finding our way together as best we might, finding something gentle and hopeful in life, some way to purposefully channel our humanity. I'm not signing up to a fight!"

"I see," she replied, her voice chill and remote. "Then since we have the steward of the feast present with us, shall we come to terms? Have you the lists I supplied, of our requirements?"

William rose to his feet and fetched the scroll from the pile on John's table. He had taken in its contents and could answer to it with convincing familiarity.

Wearily, an hour later, the abbot made his carefully courteous farewells of both ladies. They wanted to make a thorough inspection of the area where the marriage vows would be made, the refectory in which the feast would take place, and the abbey church where High Mass would follow the nuptials. John sent Brother Tom in search of Francis to be their escort; he took his leave of them with all pleasant kindness at his door – but declined to go beyond it, and left them to begin their inspections alone, with the promise that Francis would find them without delay. And he shut the door.

"You have to admit," said William, "she has a point."

"I do not," replied the abbot, shortly. He glared at William. "Hannah is a decent girl. She and Gervase love one another. Her family are good people. She deserves a chance. *And* – if you meant that as a joke, it isn't funny." His eyes blazed at William, but then he stopped himself and half-turned away. He took a deep breath and started again, more quietly: "Anyway, what about you? Haven't you got something to do? Doesn't Cormac need you?"

William grinned. He knew a man doing his best when he saw one. He made himself scarce.

John closed his eyes, counted to ten, prayed silently and fervently to remain courteous and patient, then turned his mind to the early arrival of the bishop. Skirting the court to avoid Lady Bonvallet now deep in conversation with his prior, he crossed to the guesthouse to tackle the beginning of their Visitation.

By some miracle of divine kindness, though Bishop Eric spent time with Abbot John in the afternoon, having amply lunched, and had some searching questions to ask about what John considered to be the strengths and weaknesses of this community and his own fulfilment of his role within it, the bishop felt sufficiently wearied by his journey to retire early, stating a preference to eat in privacy in the guesthouse. John took the opportunity to take his supper in the abbot's house in William's company. He felt he owed William that honour, as his guest and in thanks for his help. Besides that, it had not been an easy day, and in William's company he felt completely accepted – that here was one soul who never asked him to give an account of himself, but had the perception simply to understand.

Over supper, he told William something of his time with the bishop in the afternoon. He expressed bemusement at the distinctly odd equerry, who had urged him to smile and let slip his hidden sunshine. He took note of the wariness in William's eyes as he considered the man – "Don't trust him, John." He thought back on their encounter with Lady Florence Bonvallet and her mother, but decided no good could come of mulling over that, and left it alone. And then they ate in companionable silence.

"John… I've a kindness to beg of you."

The abbot looked up from his dinner. William seemed unsettled, he thought, out of sorts. "And it is?"

"I wondered – I do appreciate why the answer should be 'no' – but… could I – may I – come to Chapter in the morning?"

Abbot John finished chewing his mouthful of food, but he was already shaking his head before he spoke. "I'm afraid it does have to be 'no'," he said. "Chapter must remain sacrosanct for the community. It has to be that way. You have considerable freedom while you're here – to be with us in the cloister, sit with the community at Compline and in the early morning. We recognize our special relationship with you; but there must also be boundaries. And Chapter is for the brethren. Anyway, Bishop Eric may well be there, and anyone dressed as a layman would stick out like a sore thumb. I am so sorry. Why did you want to come?"

William toyed with his broken bread. "I suppose... I just wanted to hear something honest and wholesome and good. It's been a strange day. The equerry, the Bonvallets. They have their point of view, but I feel... sort of ... besmirched."

John nodded, understanding, sympathy in his eyes. "I can believe it."

"I wanted to listen to the abbot's Chapter." William spoke quietly, and John felt the containment of his spirit, the way the man kept himself held inside, furled. The world corroded him, perhaps.

"Thank you for the compliment," said John with a smile. "I assure you there are not that many men over-eager to wait upon my wisdom. I am so sorry to deny you access. Sometimes..." He reached for the carafe of ale, and poured a little into his ale-pot to enjoy with the remnants of his cheese. "... it's not unknown for men to fall asleep in my Chapter talks. These summer days it can be stuffy in there. Fresh air is helpful for staying awake, and good for us anyway. The door – not the entrance from the covered way, the little one handy for the infirmarians and anyone coming down from the farm – sometimes we leave it open on a sunny day. It's nice to hear the birds sing. I should think we'd be likely to leave it open tomorrow."

He saw his friend's face relax into gratitude and amusement.

There was this nook out of the wind's way, tucked between the bellying out of the octagonal chapter house and the buttressed wall of the main body of the church. Here William sat on the tufting grass, smelling the fragrance of lavender, sage and rosemary growing there. Herbs were planted everywhere at St Alcuin's – because they were useful and beautiful, healing and fragrant, low maintenance and extremely easy to grow. Absently, he stretched out his hand and rubbed the leaves of the lavender... the rosemary... breathing in the clean, wholesome scent.

Screened from view in this discreet cleft, he listened to Father Gilbert reading the chapter of the Rule set for today, his voice carrying out through the small door that this morning stood wide open, propped back with a rock.

"'Behold, here I am'," Benedict quoted Psalm 33. And Father Gilbert concluded the portion set: "'Behold, in his loving kindness the Lord shows us the way of life.'"

William was by now familiar with the effect the place had on him, and experienced without surprise the curious reaching forth, the yearning hunger that called from the very depths of his viscera to the unknown blue mystery of the infinite. *Amen*, his soul in silence saluted the words.

And then, what he wanted to hear: Abbot John addressed the sons of his house.

"In loving kindness, the Lord shows us the way of life. My brothers, opposing contrasts are often used to guide us. One such is *perfecta caritas foras mittit timorem* – perfect love casts out fear. What an interesting opposition. At first thought we incline to perceive hatred as opposed to love. Yet often hatred turns out to be wounded or distorted love, the result of abuse and rejection. It's a steep task, turning hatred to love, certainly – but the true opposition is fear. You cannot love where you fear – you *cannot*. Fear is inherently self-concerned, where love of its nature looks outwards, self-forgetful. Fear wants to get away where love wants to connect.

"Thinking of kindness, then, of loving kindness – I asked myself, for our guidance, the deepening of our wisdom – what is the opposite of kindness. The first thing that springs to mind is cruelty, naturally enough. Or meanness – mean-spiritedness, maybe. But cruelty... well... it is, you might say, a *secondary* thing. A fruit, not a root. The same with meanness. They are what we see. They are the behaviour, not the attitude.

"Tentatively, I want to propose to you, the root attitude in opposition to loving kindness is scorn – contempt.

"Kindness sees vulnerability, sees someone at a loss or disadvantage, and reaches out to shelter, to help. Kindness sees where someone is hurt or angry, and wants to listen, to understand; if it may be, to heal.

"Scorn sees the same things and sneers. Scorn turns away where kindness turns towards. Contempt sees someone struggling or out of their depth, and blames them. Contempt sees someone angry, smarting under an injustice perhaps, and punishes them. Above all, kindness draws people together into community, where scornful contempt isolates and divides them, keeps them forever apart.

"Christ was of no account, once. He was the child of a poor woman, born in shame, homeless. He was a prisoner brought to stand and answer for his words – he who had said, 'Tear down this temple and in three days I will build it again.' He, the healer, nailed to the cross, attracted derision – 'Messiah? Save yourself!'

"He died. But when he rose again, he didn't come back with a list drawn up of his enemies. Even in dying, what he said was, 'Father, forgive them – they don't know what they're doing.' He understood, you see. Even then.

"There's a fair amount about scorn in the Gospels. I'm thinking of the older brother of the prodigal, of the Pharisee and the Publican, of Simon the Pharisee and the woman who anointed the feet of Jesus, among others. We identify hypocrisy as the sin Jesus spoke out against – but just like cruelty, hypocrisy is a secondary thing. Hypocrisy, like cruelty, proceeds from contempt. The Pharisee held the publican in absolute contempt – as did the older brother regard the returning prodigal. He scorned him. And Simon the Pharisee looked down on the woman of ill repute; she was beneath him. Or so he thought. He made the mistake of expecting Jesus would look at her in the same way. Contempt belittles people, sees them as nothing, as insignificant, where kindness restores dignity, helps people grow.

"There's something going on here about the predilection for always being right that afflicts religious people. Wanting to be right and feeling guilty and ashamed when we get things wrong. Anxious to be in the right, we hold in utter contempt those who fail, who fall below the standards we have set. We make them into a ladder we climb, thinking to elevate ourselves. But, in heaven's name – doesn't everybody make mistakes? Isn't that how we learn? Should we not shelter our fallen brothers with kindness? Should we not overlook their follies and lift them up gently when they stumble? Guilt, shame, contempt – this becomes a morass of rancour feeding off itself. It's a knot you can untangle only with kindness.

"Kindness. Such a homely, ordinary thing at first glance. But so majestic, so spacious; the thumbprint of a generous God. 'In loving kindness, the Lord shows us the way of life.'"

William stayed where he was in the silence that followed these words. He explored the perimeter of the familiar sinkhole – shame – at his well-defended core. He thought of the derision with which he so easily dismissed men he judged to be weak or mediocre. They drew from him not kindness but contempt. He knew how scornful he could be. He bent his head, quite still, except that the fingers of his left hand strayed among the blades of grass where he sat, plucking at them as his thoughts wandered. Then as he heard the abbot open the business of the meeting, asking for the confessions of the novices, William crept from his hiding place and stole away, keeping close to the church wall where he could not be observed from the chapter house. It would be, he thought, a breach of trust to eavesdrop on the defencelessness of brothers confessing to one another, and on the private concerns of the community. He had no wish to pry.

He went into the cloister, crossed the garth all blossoming in the flowers of spring, going through to the far side of the cloister, the refectory door, and from there out to the abbey court. He thought Bishop Eric, whom he wished to avoid, would be in Chapter with the community, so he took the chance to find something to eat in the guesthouse, and to move his belongings out to a more discreet lodging, out from under the eye of the bishop. Near its door in the sunshine, he found the bishop's equerry seated at a garden table with some bread and ale.

The man raised his hand against the morning light, and offered a jocund smile. "Here's a merry thing!" he exclaimed, showing William a small spider who had been spinning her thread, using the corner of the table to attach the web she had strung between its silvered oak and the rosemary. It glinted in the sunshine. "Look!" The equerry laughed as he trapped one of her legs beneath his finger, detaching it from her body. He did it to a second leg, a third, a fourth, two more. William stood immobile, watching the futile movement of the last two legs. Smiling, the equerry took these away one by one, leaving only her body and the tiny threads of her scattered legs. Then, laughing, he reached down and brushed the web away.

William stepped forward to the table, neither looking at nor speaking to the man. With delicate care, he lifted the still body of the garden spider, placed her on the sunwarmed flag of stone where he stood, and with one decisive movement crushed her absolutely. He did not turn his head to see if the equerry was still smiling. He went into the guesthouse; but there he walked past the table where food had been set out for the taking. He took the stairs two at a time and retrieved his bag and cloak from the bed where he'd been sleeping. The house had a kitchen of its own, and by that way he made his exit, to avoid being seen by LePrique or, for that matter, having to look at him. Quietly and swiftly he walked along under the trees to the stables, and climbed the wooden ladder into the big hayloft. He swung himself up through the hatch, and crossed the boarded space, strewn with fragrant grass and seeds. Mice, he knew, would confine their activities mainly to the floor. He climbed onto the hay pile, to the very back of the loft, crouching to make himself a hollow close against the wall just beneath the small window, where the scanty light would find him, he could hear what passed outside, but would be unseen should anyone come up to investigate. He wrapped his cloak around him and lay down, curling up into the nest he had made. There he lay quite still, thinking of the bishop, the equerry, the spider. Even wrapped in his cloak and bedded in the hay, he felt cold now, not entirely sure it had been the right choice to come back here again.

Chapter Two

"So, you've met Florence. Would you like to be there when Hannah and Gervase come to see me? Is that helpful?"

William shook his head. "The path I've taken has created consequences – as all decisions do. It's not realistic to hope a man can be what I've been and do as I've done without incurring some associated curtailments and forfeits. That's not how life is. I think, especially while Bishop Eric is here, there should be no question that I am here too. LePrique was never acquainted with me, neither was Florence, so I'm hoping we can get away with that; but Hannah knows me well. It's risky to rely even on the community for discretion, though I think we can. They will have the sense – I hope – to give away nothing of my presence. Let's just leave it like that. Maybe I'll have a chance to observe Gervase in some casual setting; but I do believe I must concentrate on fading and vanishing while I'm here. I've moved my bits and pieces into your hayloft, you know. Out of sight. Best keep things that way."

John saw the force of this, and William set off for the kitchens, for Brother Conradus to approve the list he and Cormac had made of provisions still to be obtained in the near future.

"Will you need me?" asked Brother Tom, setting out the chairs for John's visitors.

"Er... no. Probably not. They're only coming to talk; they won't need feeding. I'll need you this evening, because Bishop

Eric will be dining with me here, and possibly Brainard too – I'm not quite sure of the protocol; if it would be expected that Brainard eats always in the guesthouse or sometimes with me. I think I'd better ask Francis; he'll know. And I believe Gervase Bonvallet's brothers – Hubert and Percival – are coming up this afternoon. Conradus said they have several casks of special wine from France, and they want to move it now so it has time to settle before it's broached. So I guess they'd better stay for supper too. The daylight lasts to see them safely home afterwards at this time of year. They've only got to ride a mile or two beyond the village. Francis will eat with us, and I think maybe Father Gilbert. He can talk to them about the music for the wedding, and he… well, he comes of an aristocratic family. He and Francis will fit in with them better than I do. I did ask William, but he said he'd make himself scarce while his Lordship is with us. So we may be a party of seven here this evening, but nothing that needs your attention during the day."

"Have I your permission, then, to be out with Brother Stephen?"

"Remind me of what you were doing."

"We need to go up onto t' moor to gather a goodly lot of bracken for a first layer under the hayricks when we build them – it keeps the damp from the hay so it doesn't rot, and the rats don't like it. We always spread a thick layer of it first, but it's tough work gathering it – rough old stuff. It's a help if there's two of us."

"But…" John frowned, puzzled. "Wouldn't you get it in during the autumn?"

"Aye, we do. But we ran so short of hay and straw for animal bedding last year, because so much of what we had went mouldy with all that rain. We had bracken set by for when we built the ricks, but we used it up. It doesn't matter. Bracken doesn't harbour damp like grass. If we gather it now, it'll dry out as much

44

as it needs to and be ready for when we fetch the hay in. And Brother Walafrid said, would we get some for him to make his next lot of soap."

John hesitated.

"I don't have to go," admitted Tom, but his abbot perceived the moral effort it cost him to say it, and he laughed.

"No, that's all right – of course you can. But will you call by the kitchen and see to it that Brother Conradus brings some cakes and wine for the bishop this afternoon? And make sure he's aware of how many we'll be, eating here tonight."

Tom grinned cheerfully. "Aye, I will! I should be back by the afternoon, anyway. We'll take some bread and cheese with us, and go this morning. I'll look around the ditches on the farm as well, see if there's any meadowsweet blooming yet, to strew in here for your supper guests. Bit early in the year yet, but I'll see what there is."

John felt his enthusiasm, the tug of the outdoors on his spirit, and was glad he'd not required him to be confined inside, patiently waiting on his abbot's guests.

"I'm grateful to you, Tom," he said. "Thank you for helping me and steering me through. I know it's not easy."

"Nay, it's a privilege – a joy, really," replied his esquire. "Don't fret; I'll not be long away."

No sooner had Tom left by the cloister door, bound for the farm and the open moorland that rose above it, than John heard the knock on the door to the abbey court, heralding the arrival of Hannah and Gervase.

"Welcome!" He gestured them in.

Gervase, without really thinking about it, took his seat in one of the two chairs available that John indicated. Hannah paused, then changed direction and chose to sit instead on one of the two low stools, the only other seats. She left the remaining chair for the abbot. He smiled at her. "Thank you." He took his seat in the chair she left him. "Now, then. How's everything going? All well? Happy? Looking forward to it?"

Hannah grinned. Gervase looked at him as if John had lost his mind.

"It's a nightmare," he said. "My mother – you have no idea! When I'm by myself, it all seems straightforward. When I'm with Hannah, I come home to myself, I start to be who I really am. Everything falls into place. Then my mother starts up, and by the time she's finished I'm overflowing with shame and guilt and misery, worried that I'm ruining Hannah's life and destroying my children's chances of happiness, disgracing the family name and disappointing my father –"

"Has he said so?" John interrupted.

"My father? He's said barely a word. Shrugged, looked away, muttered things along the lines of 'On your own head be it', and retreated into silence. Yes, if I'm honest, I think I probably have disappointed him. But then again, I think there may have been something inevitable about that from the day I was born. I'm not like him. I don't think like him. I let him down by being the lad I am. But what can I do about that? I have tried. I've done what I can to please them. But this… I really want this, Father. I really do. I think my family will not actually disown us. I believe my father has plans to give us a small farm of our own a few miles away. He just doesn't want us anywhere near him and my mother. He won't be unkind. He won't disinherit me. So long as we keep our distance and don't do anything to embarrass the family."

John let the bleak chill of these thoughts settle into his marrow like wet snow.

"My family – my ma and da, my brothers – they are happy for us," said Hannah softly. "And my da and my brother will help us if we do have our own farm. Help us get started."

John smiled at her. "And are you looking forward to your wedding day, Hannah?"

"Aye! Indeed I am! I know what Gervase's family thinks of me – they've made it plain. But they've been good to us even so, Father. I mean, look, they've stumped up for a grand feast, nothing spared. And I'm so excited about the minstrels – there's to be jugglers. And a lady to play a harp. I think that will be beautiful. A great big harp, it's to be. She'll have to bring it on a cart! I... I think – I hope – it'll be a very special day, Father John; don't you?"

Hannah spoke bravely, but he could see she had lost much of the bounce and sparkle natural to her in these recent weeks. He remembered the day he had walked up the last few miles to St Alcuin's, returning to take up the abbacy after a year away. He'd met her out with her goats, waving joyously when she recognized him walking up the track, running down to greet him, enfolding him in an exuberant, affectionate hug. She looked more restrained now.

"It will be a joyous day," he said firmly. "All the angels singing. You seem to me very well suited to one another. I think the way lies clear for you to be happy. The gift of a farm is a generous prospect indeed. And if that comes about, though I doubt we can offer much help in the way of labour, don't hesitate to ask us if you need advice – Brother Stephen, Brother Thomas; there's not much they don't know.

"It's not – this discouragement – it's not a bad thing, really, you know. To enter into a marriage, well, it's in accord with our human nature, but even so it's wise to be sure. Much as, though there are monasteries up and down the breadth of the land, even so, when a young man comes to us and says he has a calling, we test it, we probe it, we go slowly. It's not a thing to go into lightly. Still, it is a blessed thing, and I for one will have a heart overflowing with joy when you tie the knot."

Gervase looked at him curiously. Something of his mother there, thought the abbot, unerringly detecting the slightly false note in the fulsome reassurances of angels singing and a joyous heart, but forbearing from comment. John hoped they would find contentment in taking their way together. It didn't seem entirely likely, somehow. But they believed in their love. Who was he to blight it any further than it already had been? Let them take their chances. Especially seeing as they already had two children.

"In a community like ours," he said, "we have all kinds of men from many different family backgrounds. They come with a variety of assumptions about life, all quickly overturned. Our rule of thumb is to remember that each one is doing his best, each one has his struggles. To give one another the benefit of the doubt. To cultivate a sense of humour. To think twice before making any sort of rebuke. And to be kind. Vocation is noble, but the charcoal beds of everyday life are what filter and refine it from its original condition into something pure and useable.

"A marriage is a community as well – the two of you, your children, the lads and lasses who work together with you in your house and on your fields. Community begins with two, I suppose."

They heard him with courtesy; they had little to ask, and no comment to make. Like most who came to see him, they regarded him with a certain degree of awe, and tremendous respect. John found this almost unbelievable, but accepted the reality of it. And he supposed he relied on it to make his life manageable. If everyone who came into the abbot's house felt free to expand in his company and chat away freely, not much would get done. If they were shy in his presence, at least it kept the conversation shorter than it might have been, and left more time for the next in line.

After they had gone, he sat for a while in silence and stillness, thinking about the young couple and the picture they had sketched for him. He felt uneasy about their future. He imagined the difference it could have made if Gervase's mother and father had taken delight in their love. He thought of Gervase saying his father wouldn't "be unkind", meaning nothing more than that he would not be entirely estranged. He wondered if Gervase had ever really known what kindness looked like, before he knew Hannah.

"Oh God, Father of us all," he whispered into the silence, "breathe your kindness like a fragrance into our lives. Raise us up to be sons of God. Lift us out of the dust of half-measures and ingrained meanness. Raise us up. Breathe your kindness through our lives."

He sat a moment longer, then on the impulse of sudden resolve left his atelier and went along the cloister and up the day stairs to the novitiate, in search of Father Theodore. He hesitated at the door – which stood ajar – hearing familiar voices inside. He realized that occupying his morning with the wedding couple had left the bishop at a loose end. Evidently he'd thought he might as well get on with his Visitation.

"And what do you think, Brother Robert" – this was the bishop – "of Peter Lombard's *Libri Quatuor Sententiarum*? I think I want to ask you in particular what you think of William of Ockham's commentary thereon."

John could easily picture Father Theodore physically ceasing to breathe as this question was put. To take a novice as essentially clueless as Brother Robert into the treacherous territory of borderline heresy seemed hardly fair. Sure enough, it was Theo's voice, not Robert's, next heard in reply – low, respectful.

"Ah, your Lordship! Ockham's commentary runs into ten volumes, as you know. We have touched upon them, but not covered them – yet – in depth. Our studies this year have focused on the theology of the Eucharist. But we have discussed Ockham's razor, Brother Robert, have we not?"

"Really?" The bishop again; though a second voice murmuring, LePrique's, urging a reminder. Evidently at this point Brother

49

Robert was forgetting to smile. The bishop once more: "Tell me what you have learned of *lex parsimoniae*, then, Brother Robert – of Ockham's razor."

"He... it's... I think... um... it's about doing your best to keep things simple. Not complicating everything. Because a razor is narrow and sharp, and cuts through the – er – through the ..." Yes. John could well imagine what Theo might originally have said. "He – Ockham – he thought that you could get in a muddle if you made too many assumptions. Better to start small."

"*Entia non sunt multiplicanda praeter necessitatem.*" Brother Cassian, having the temerity to interrupt, albeit quietly and with humility. He must have seen Robert struggling, and the approach to novitiate studies they were used to with Theo could better be described as a free-for-all than wait-until-you're-spoken-to.

"Aha!" exclaimed his Lordship. "Go on, then – say more?"

"It means you don't exceed what is necessary, in your thinking," Brother Cassian explained. "That if you have two explanations, you should ditch the fancy one in favour of the plain one. Unless the fancy one is for some reason better. So, you take the best one, but always the simplest best one. Not try to choose something complicated just to show off and look clever. And you should assume things are just natural and straightforward unless you have reason to think otherwise. So if you hear a bump in the night from the next cell, you assume someone has fallen out of bed, not that they're wrestling with an angel. Because it's more likely, even if it could in principle be an angel."

"Very good," approved his Lordship. "That's about right. And what about Ockham's theology of the Eucharist – either of you? Any of you?"

"He... he said..." – this voice belonged to the obsessively diligent Brother Felix, so John had good hopes what he was about to hear might well be correct – "that Christ's body is truly contained in all of the host, and in all of its parts at once. That the reality of Christ present succeeds the humble nature of bread. There isn't an interim stage when it's both, when both natures somehow blend in together. It's bread, then it's the host of Christ's presence."

"*Very* good!" The bishop sounded impressed, though from what he could detect of Brainard's murmuring, Brother Felix was falling down on the job of keeping his smile in place as well.

"What else have you learned about the theology of the Eucharist? What does Quidort say – and Aquinas?"

John put his hand to the door, thinking this could well be a good moment to interrupt, but paused as he heard Felix begin to speak again. "He – Quidort – did not accept the interpretation given by Aquinas, your Lordship. John Quidort spoke of the nature of the bread being not supplanted by the presence of Christ, but being drawn into the greater being of the *Logos* – the holy Word, the mystical presence of Christ who is there in all the cosmos, in us who make our communion with the living Christ, in the bread, in the body."

John saluted this with a silent cheer, and thought Theo must feel profoundly relieved and gratified to know that at least one of his lads had been listening. But when the bishop said, "And you, young man? What are your own beliefs about the Eucharist?" he judged this the right moment to cut in. He didn't want any of his novices arraigned before an ecclesiastical court for heresy. And it could happen. Not everyone applied Ockham's razor and assumed basic lack of sophistication and natural stupidity. Some would leap with alacrity to conclude evidence of a subtle and subversive mind at work in sly undermining of the authority of Holy Church, and never stop to ask how likely that was. John pushed open the door.

"Ah! My lord bishop! And Monsieur LePrique. Good morrow to you both. I hope you are finding our novices come up to the mark."

Thank you, moved Theo's lips in silent mime as John glanced at him across the tense circle of robed men.

"They seem well versed indeed," replied the bishop, all geniality. "I was just enquiring about their own views on transubstantiation."

John smiled. Out of the corner of his eye he saw Brainard nod in satisfaction and encouragement at this. "My lord, do not forget this is only Yorkshire," said the abbot. "Not Avignon, nor yet the Vatican. I hold Father Theodore's scholarly ability and considerable intellect in the highest esteem; but mine cannot compare. Some of what our novices have learned will be from my Chapter addresses and homilies at Mass. If you find any fault, come back to me, of your charity. It will be my own shortcoming."

Though he allowed himself to be diverted from too careful an assessment of their theological orthodoxy, the bishop still persisted with his questions until the welcome sound of the bell ringing for the midday office brought him to a halt. The abbot and the novice master detached him from their novices and flanked him in an escort down the day stairs to the south transept of the church, allowing the young men to flow around and ahead of them. They both felt a sense of having navigated their way across the treacherous, icy waters of a winter stream.

After chapel, as the brothers departed for the frater, Abbot John remained in his stall. Father Theodore crossed the choir and sat in the prior's place alongside him. "Why did you come up this morning?" he asked, in a discreet undertone that respected the solemnity of the choir. "You were looking for me, not the bishop, weren't you?"

John nodded. He didn't want to have this conversation here, but if they went back to his house they'd be late for the midday meal, and if they set off for the refectory they'd run into Bishop Eric.

"It's Gervase and Hannah, Theo; I'm worried about them."

"Because –?"

"There's such wide variance in their backgrounds and opposition from Gervase's family. And, you know how it is. The aristocracy have a hundred and one ways of disposing of people like Hannah. She's walking into a lions' den. If he ever tires of her…"

Theo considered this, his face sober. He sighed. "Well, it's true. But might we not have said the same of William and Madeleine? If ever a match was ill-advised, it must have been theirs. Yet from the whispers that reach me, they are happy together. And your efforts to stop them were made with the best of intentions but only made them miserable. Even if the ground of this union is shaky to walk on, if Hannah can't see that for herself, what's to be done? Seems to me this is one of those things where you have to trust in God and not interfere, Father."

John accepted this, with reluctance. "Aye. You're right. I suppose you're right. Very well, then; I'll let it be." He shook it off him and looked at his novice master with a smile. "Your lads gave a good account of themselves to the bishop, did they not?"

"Indeed they did. Good thing he came today and not yesterday. They were all in the kitchen learning to make pastry."

"What? Why?"

"Brother Conradus will need some extra help for the wedding. He asked if they could all come down, to see who had some aptitude."

"No! Tell me you're joking! Making pastry? With the bishop breathing down our necks? They need to be hard at it, Theo, earnest and diligent. Or at least looking like they are. Pastry!"

"Oh, I don't know." Theo smiled. "I think it's good for them to try something other than book work once in a while. I've had them down in the pottery learning how to make bowls. I've sent them to Brother Walafrid a time or two, to learn how to make tinctures and poultices – basic medicine."

"Aye, well that's useful! That's worthwhile. But – pastry?"

"So speaks an infirmarian," retorted his novice master. "But listen – while I think of it – Conradus tells me you've sent for his mother to come and work alongside him in the kitchen for the Bonvallet wedding. Have I understood him right? You didn't, did you?"

"For sure. Yes, I did. Is that – is there a problem?"

"Who suggested this? Not Conradus. Oh, don't tell me – this was William's bright idea, wasn't it! John, what are you thinking of? We can't have a woman working here in the cloister!"

John hesitated, disconcerted. "She's not... not a *woman* exactly. This is Brother Conradus's mother."

"What?"

"I mean – well, she won't pose any kind of temptation, will she? She must be near enough my age, and she'll be a little roly-poly comfortable farm wench. She... well, she'll be like Brother Conradus but a lot older. What's wrong with that? What trouble are you expecting? What could possibly go wrong? Nobody's going to fall in love with Brother Conradus's *mother*!"

Theo ran his hand across his scalp. "John, didn't you say when Madeleine came here that there's always trouble when women mix in with the community?"

"Oh yes, but" – John waved his hand in dismissal of this – "Madeleine came to *live* here. Rose will only be here a matter of a fortnight. What problems can she cause in a fortnight, for heaven's sake?"

"I've no idea," said Theo. "Let's wait and see. But I'll have to think twice about the novices helping in the kitchen. Right, then. Shall we have something to eat?"

They walked to the frater in silence.

✠   ✠   ✠

54

In the afternoon, John took the bishop across to the school. One of the few decisions he had made by himself in these first difficult months of his abbacy, was a recent transplanting of Brother Damian from the infirmary and Brother Josephus from various manual tasks, to work in the school. Brother Cassian helped out when his novitiate studies permitted. This dispensation proved to be happy and effective. Occasionally Father Gilbert came in to teach them the rudiments of music, and Father Clement to watch over their penmanship. The boys had evidently been warned of their inspection, and John saw their abnormally angelic behaviour as evidence of a supportive attitude towards their schoolmasters – from which he took encouragement. The bishop was satisfied with what he saw and made no rigorous inquisition. He next asked to visit the checker.

"Perhaps in the morning?" suggested John. He thought it more than likely William would be there, and such a meeting ought to be avoided if at all possible. Even in layman's clothing and sporting a beard, William was hard to disguise. "I'm hoping your Lordship will dine with me this evening, and I don't wish to tire you."

"Nonsense! Not at all!" The bishop laughed at the suggestion. "I'm as fresh as a daisy. Let's go now." As they walked across the court, the abbot discoursed as loudly as he dared without sounding strange, making frequent use of "your Lordship" and "my lord bishop" in his conversation. As they neared the checker, he halted, turning back toward the main buildings of the abbey, gesturing up towards the crenellations atop the west range. "I believe we have to do some leadwork, your Lordship," he said in a stentorian voice, inventing wildly. "I don't suppose you can really see from here, but we've had some incursion of water into one or two of the cells. Along there. No – a little further."

The bishop lifted his hand to shade his eyes from the sun as he scanned the meaningless vista. John heard a slight sound from the direction of the checker, and hoped he'd sufficiently advertised their imminent arrival.

"Please don't concern yourself," he said in a more normal tone. "It's nothing but a small domestic matter. Below your interest, really."

In the checker, the bland innocence which met him in Brother Cormac's gaze, as that obedientiary rose to greet them, told him the stalling tactics had done the trick.

"New in post, you say?" the bishop remarked with surprise, looking up at Cormac from the immaculate accounts spread out ready for him to see. "Well, by all the saints, you're doing a marvellous job!"

The new cellarer enlarged convincingly on the state of the abbey's finances. The picture he portrayed could be summarized as "struggling with chronic poverty in this moorland wilderness, but frugal and careful and an exemplar of responsible management". Cormac, it seemed, had come a long way in three days.

Later, as he knocked on the wood of his stall with his ring for the community to rise and begin Vespers, Abbot John thought the day had passed off tolerably well so far. But he was not looking forward to the evening, with its influx of sophisticated guests.

⌗   ⌗   ⌗

Brother Tom had lit the fire even now in May. The abbey's thick stone walls meant the rooms were always cool through the summer, and bitterly cold in winter. In the evenings, a fire was always a welcome sight, cheery and hospitable, the woody fragrance a pleasant addition to any occasion.

Father Gilbert, the abbey's precentor, stood holding his hands out toward the blaze, appreciative. Abbot John stood with his prior, looking toward the door to the courtyard as he awaited the knock announcing his guests. Their desultory conversation had dried up. Francis glanced at his abbot and saw that he felt nervous. John had natural authority and character of considerable stature. He had moral conviction, deep faith and a good mind. He had compassion, quick insight, and the instinct to turn to prayer. What he lacked was sophisticated social finesse in his upbringing. The son of a soldier killed in battle and a village wise-woman who had subsisted on gifts of thanks for her success in practising the healing arts, he had grown up in poverty. Monastic life had taught him all he knew of the aristocracy, and that was not much. He could read and write when he came, knew any amount of practical and effective country lore; he had cared for sick men in the infirmary with competence, consolidating what he knew as he gained experience. In his novitiate years he had learned Latin and Greek, been required to study theology and become tolerably adept at following musical notation. But the *savoir-faire* and refinement men like Francis and Gilbert brought with them into monastic life had made little impression; they were expected for the most part to keep it to themselves. Simplicity and humility were valued above wit and urbanity. Nobody asked them to sparkle. Just now and then – and this evening was one such occasion – John wished quite desperately that he had a family background like that of his predecessor, Father Peregrine, on whose shoulders the cloak of elegant formality and propriety sat lightly and naturally, a French aristocrat born to noblesse. John knew quite well how far from polished was his own social manner. When it came to spiritual counsel, he was sure-footed; his knowledge of humanity gave him confidence. In this gathering about to eat at his table he would feel distinctly rustic. But he was grateful for Father Francis and Father Gilbert there with him, and had the strength of spirit to keep his sense of rising panic firmly in check, if not entirely quelled.

When the knock came, he stepped forward to answer, but Francis's restraining hand on his arm held him back; his esquire,

Brother Thomas, opened the door. And then Francis lifted his hand away. When John, his assurance evaporating, still did not move, Francis murmured a quiet "Yes", glancing encouragingly at his abbot, and stepped forward himself. Something in John that always observed, always took note, asked how did he do that – Francis? How did he manage to both take the lead and yet seem to hang back, to give his abbot preference? Tonight, as so often before, he silently thanked William for his shrewd judgment of men, for identifying Francis as the right man to set in the obedience of prior.

"My lord bishop," he said; "Brainard – come in. Welcome to my table." Francis had given the go-ahead for this invitation. It was proper, he'd said, for bishop and abbot sometimes to dine alone; but since Hubert and Percival Bonvallet would be with them, it would be a kind gesture to include the equerry. LePrique's social standing was greater than that of an ordinary servant. He was not a chaplain, but some courtesy should be extended in recognition of his position's status. And John had wondered, *How does he know? How does Francis always know?* At the same time seeing that Francis didn't know that he knew. He thought everyone knew. He thought it was obvious. So he made a good prior.

Hubert and Percival breezed in with a turbulence of loud geniality, and their repast got off to a good start with Conradus's excellent herb bread and consommé soup. Wine flowed freely and lubricated the conversation. The bishop tucked in with gusto. The second course balanced the piquancy of myriad salad leaves – many of them wild herbs and simples, John noticed; broadleafed plantain, rocket, young dandelion – against perfectly seasoned chicken breasts in a creamy sauce. Brother Thomas changed the wine. *How does he know which wine to serve?* John asked himself; then realized he probably didn't, but Conradus did.

"Think about it," Brainard was saying to Father Gilbert (the only person willing to listen to him now Francis was occupied in conveying just the right tempered amusement at Percival Bonvallet's recounting of his dubious social conquests), "does not a smile make every man immediately more attractive? Suppose you start the day in a sour mood. Then your brother smiles at you. Does this not instantly disperse the gloomy clouds? A smile has special powers! The sunshine you radiate reflects back to you. It makes you feel better inside. It expresses the joy of salvation. Even when nothing seems harder, nothing further from your true desires; just do it, Father... er... just do it!"

"Gilbert," said Father Gilbert quietly.

"Yes?" responded Brainard, his smile beaming encouragement; then, leaning in, "Though actually my name is Brainard. Brainard LePrique."

Somewhere in the back of his head John imagined William's impassive face, heard his dry murmur, "Aye, it would be." He watched Father Gilbert's face pucker in slight puzzlement, not following, and thought his precentor had probably had too much to drink.

"My compliments to your kitchen brother," said the bishop to Brother Thomas as he stooped to lift his Lordship's plate away. "He has excelled himself again. Oh – what's this? Fruit and cheese! Ah – figs! And some marzipan sweetmeats. And mead? My favourite!"

There came a certain mellow lull over the cheese. A contented satiety settled on the company. John felt cautiously pleased. This was going well. As conversation around the table momentarily ceased, Francis said quietly, "*Un ange passe.*"

Hubert looked across at him with the lopsided smile of a well-lubricated wit.

"*C'est peut-être l'Abbé Bé,*" he said meaningfully.

"*Puéril,*" responded Francis with a grin.

What? thought John.

"*Ou – le Père Plexe?*" offered Percival.

Francis grimaced, moved his hand in a so-so gesture. "*Religieux*," he said, "*mais dubitative.*"[1]

John looked from man to man. They were all grinning. Presumably he should be as well. He wasn't sure what to do. Latin, he knew passably well. Greek, he could just about master. But of French he had only a smattering, and that mostly what he'd picked up from Peregrine's colourful muttering in the infirmary.

"*Eh bien, peut-être ça c'est le Père Missif,*" suggested Brainard, smiling broadly.

"*Un peu trop laxiste,*" responded the bishop.

"*Ou bien, la Mère Itante,*" said Hubert – and his brother chimed in, "*qui a bien gagnée sa place au ciel!*"

The palms of John's hands began to sweat, and his belly tightened until he felt sick.

"*L'Abbé Casse?*" put forward the bishop; and, "*Un drôle d'oiseau!*" said Father Gilbert with a smile.

"Come on, Father!" LePrique turned the sunshine of his smile upon the abbot. "You give us one!" John's mouth went dry.

"*La Soeur Titude, enfin?*" LePrique roared with laughter at this contribution from Father Francis. And Gilbert came back at him: "*Mais on n'a jamais été sûr d'elle!*"

"*Ou, l'Abbé Névole?*" Percival now. His brother answered with: "*Oui – car celui-ci ne demande jamais rien!*" And they were laughing. They were all laughing, and snatching small glances in the direction of the abbot wondering why he wasn't laughing too.

"*L'Abbé Nédiction,*" said Francis, raising his goblet as if he were making a toast. And every single one of them (except John) immediately roared as one: "Ameeeeeennnnn!!"

"Ahhhh... Heheheh..." The bishop leaned forward to catch John's eye as the laughter subsided. "Not amused, Father John? Oh, come, come, come! Don't disapprove of us!"

1 If you are as bewildered as Abbot John, head across to the glossary.

Frozen, John looked back at him. He had no idea what to say. But Brainard stepped in. "Did you know," he said, "it has been put forward that people who smile actually live longer? A scowling demeanour is actually bad for your health! A smile can melt away –"

"Yes, yes, Brainard," interrupted the bishop. "Very good. No doubt it can. But maybe – oh, hark; there's the Compline bell."

"And time we were on the road," said Percival.

John registered that he was trembling so badly that he found it hard to rise convincingly from the table to take leave of them with all due courtesy; but he did it somehow, Francis sending the occasional worried glance in his direction.

Fading light and the call to worship kept all farewells brief. The bishop hurried away to make use of the reredorter before Compline began. Father Gilbert, as hebdomedarian, excused himself and set off to the choir.

Francis, Tom and John stood in the abbot's house as the bell tolled, beside the table cluttered with left-over food, goblets, crumpled napkins and plates.

"What happened?" asked Francis softly. Brother Tom darted a glance at John, permitting himself a small, rueful smile. "I think," he said, "our abbot may not speak French. As neither do I."

Involuntarily, Francis's hand rose to his mouth in horror. "I… oh, John! Holy mother of God, I am so very sorry. I never thought. I… oh, dear. What can I possibly do to make this better?"

"Kill me now?" suggested his abbot. "Oh, forget it, Francis, never mind. No – please don't faff about kneeling and making apology. We're late already, and I've had enough."

Then, recalling the bishop's equerry's exhortations and thinking there might be something in what he said, John took a deep breath, and smiled at Francis. "His Lordship looks cheerful enough, at any rate. The whole Visitation's going remarkably smoothly so far. He was very encouraging to our novices today.

Odd, that. William didn't seem to like him in the least. Hadn't a good word to say for him."

"Aye, well – that's nowt fresh, is it?" said Brother Tom. "William has a jaundiced and suspicious view of the whole human race. I'd not set too much store by his opinions if I were you. Come on, Father John. Let's go to chapel. I'll clear this lot up later."

John nodded. Still determined to be cheerful and put the awful evening behind him, he asked, "Did you get the bracken you wanted? Did the day go well?"

"It did," responded his esquire. "We'll need to go at least once more, though. We got what we could stack on the small cart, but it's only half what we need, if that. I'll find a chance when there's a quiet moment later in the week."

A quiet moment, thought the abbot. *Remind me what those are, again.* But he knew it would sound sour, so he didn't say it. They went into the peaceful vaulted shadows of the abbey church, and he felt more glad than he could say to let the gentle measure of Compline's chanting take his day down to rest.

✠   ✠   ✠

After Chapter, the abbot received Bishop Eric in his lodging. Respectfully, he invited his Visitor to be seated, and offered refreshment from the jug of small beer Brother Thomas had judged suitable to partake at this time of day. The bishop enquired and, discovering it not to be wine, decided not to bother.

"I am getting the drift of your spiritual teaching among the brethren, Abbot John," began the bishop. "I like your friendly, conversational, familiar style. A good stratagem – especially with the novices. Makes them feel comfortable and at ease, no doubt – the homely approach. Yes – yes, I can see there is merit in it. To draw upon personal experience; a simple faith, a simple Gospel.

Just believe and all will be well; no need to think, just keep on from day to day."

John did not recognize in this description anything he could recall having said, but could see such a comment would hardly be welcome. Besides, the bishop was only warming up.

"But now," went on his Lordship, "perhaps the time has come to dig deeper. You have been in post for – what – eighteen months? During that time no doubt you have made extensive study in theology, maybe even begun to write a book. Have you?"

John could hardly begin to frame a reply to this. The last eighteen months. Turmoil. Struggle. The turbulent days of William's brief residence with them. The anguish of his mother's death and the outrage of Madeleine's violation. The inner turmoil of trying to find his feet in navigating some kind of compassionate passage through William's departure and marriage, trying to hold on to at least the hem of Christ's garment of integrity and truth, not lose his way in monastic vocation in making himself spacious enough to accept William as his brother-in-law. The massive loss – then restoration – of the community's income. The last eighteen months… write a book? He could now.

"I…" He could see Bishop Eric waiting upon his reply. "I have never imagined myself as a writer," he said. "I… don't know." That this sounded nothing like the man of intellect and acumen he was supposed to be, John felt all too keenly aware. The bishop frowned.

"Hmm. I see. No doubt you have kept records of your Chapter talks? No? Why not? I was going to suggest you start there. You could move on now from these homely little encouragements to something of real calibre. Something stronger. I know you will have thought it fitting to begin gently – shrewd, very shrewd – but I judge the community would be ready now for you to beef things up a bit. Some meaty theology. Something wider and deeper. Richer. More inspiring. Something substantial."

Silence lengthened between them, as the bishop looked expectantly at the abbot. John wondered if he could even begin to confess that he poured his heart and soul into what he offered the community in Chapter. That there was no more to give, no more inside him, beyond what he already put before them.

"Of course, your Lordship," he said humbly. "I'll do my best."

Nothing improved after that. Bishop Eric wanted to hear about John's vision for enlarging St Alcuin's prestige in the local community – by which he meant the aristocracy; nobody else's esteem mattered much. What plans had he for musical development, for creating a circle of debate, for building on such reputation for scholarly achievement as they had?

"I always thought," mused the bishop, "your predecessor should have written a book. Abbot Columba was a man of real depth, true intelligence. Nobody like him. A man of stature. He had a quality of greatness about him. I should think you have your work cut out to step into his shoes. Well, never mind. I'm thinking of writing a book myself, you know. About the ethical realization of the theology of transubstantiation applied to the political structures of the nation. What do you think?"

John swallowed. "If you do that," he said, "it would be an honour indeed if you would permit us to make a copy for our library. Oh – have you seen our library yet? No? Well, while you are here, I'll show you round. And I wondered if today you might like to see the work we do in the pottery. And visit our infirmary."

"The infirmary – no," retorted the bishop. "I am a man of too much consequence to risk contagion. And I doubt your old men in their dotage are worth examination. But it would be diverting to take a look at your little pottery."

The abbot smiled at him, though he did not find it easy. "I'll ask Father Francis to take you," he said. "Brother Thomas – would you find Father Prior and ask him to come *directly*."

The abbot's esquire, who knew a man at the end of his rope when he saw one, vanished without a word, and returned with all speed, Francis hurrying along in his wake.

In an ideal world, the abbot thought, Lady Florence Bonvallet would not follow hot on the heels of Bishop Eric into his life. When the community had elected him abbot, he had grasped the solemnity of the charge – a weight of spiritual responsibility that no man dare take lightly. But he had not appreciated the extent to which he would be tasked with diplomatically fending off constitutionally difficult people determined to bend him to their point of view. To resist without offending was not always easy. He acknowledged that, as he saw the bishop out of his house with a promise to see him later in the day, and opened the door to Lady Bonvallet, he felt somewhat buffeted; like a man trying to keep his feet in very slippery mud and a gale force wind.

"Good morrow, my lady; come in. I trust you are well? Your mother is well? Not with you today?" He did what he could to set aside the persisting irritation at Bishop Eric's remarks about his abbot's Chapters, let it go, let it fade. He smiled at Lady Bonvallet. She looked at him. She herself was evidently not in a smiling mood.

"It is a sore trial to me, this marriage," she began without preamble as she took her seat. "I think Gervase must be out of his mind. What will he do when he tires of her and he bears a duty to a fat, coarse woman and a rabble of Mitchell spawn? How will he live cut off from all his friends? He doesn't know what he's doing; he's little more than a boy. He hasn't the maturity to understand what will be the consequences of his action. He's fallen for a pleasing manner and an ample bosom, poor silly lad. It'll wear off. It should never have come to this. You're a man of position, you should surely see how inappropriate this is. Why haven't you stopped him? Where is your good counsel when we depend on you? And *don't* you tell me it's his own fault!"

Abbot John sat quietly, concentrating on keeping his hands folded loosely in his lap, not allowing their grip to tighten, merely feeling skin against skin, holding himself steady in the aliveness of his human hands. Someone putting words into his mouth, unfairly attributing to him opinions he had not expressed, incensed him without fail. But he would not be drawn by this. As a young man, fiery temper had made him impetuous, often hasty in his responses, quick to snap back. Several years in St Alcuin's infirmary serving the aged and the sick had schooled him to forbearance. He considered the glare in which he was fixed, striving to set aside his indignation and feel his way to some answer that would keep faith with Hannah and Gervase without deepening this adamant antagonism. Then he saw no reply would be necessary; Lady Bonvallet was entirely equal to the task of supplying her own.

"It is not *his* doing, it's *hers*. Hannah is the one at the root of this mischief. She has seen her chance, scheming minx. Hannah has her eye on our family money – and on our name. She wants to get her hands on something she wasn't born to. This is no true marriage, and it never will be. You mark my words, five years down the line we shall see ruin and despair. A young man with so much promise, such a deal of care and wealth invested in him, brought down to failure and discontentment by a foolish choice like this. A marriage is not about love; it's a strategic decision. It has to be carefully calculated for a long-term result. It is more than a stepping stone; it is a foundation. You can build a whole dynasty on the rock of a shrewd marriage. And that's not what this is."

At some point, as she held him in the grip of her baleful stare, Lady Bonvallet recognized in the abbot something she knew from long familiarity with her husband. He had stopped listening. Though this aggravated her, since she felt he should be paying attention to what was both important and unquestionably right, she knew from long experience that distracted look opened a chance to ask for almost anything. She took it.

"Then there are all these guests arriving, and where shall we put the musicians? The minstrels. We cannot house all comers;ours is only a modest manor. They will have to come straight here. You have plenty of room. I will send them on as soon as they arrive. It will only be for a few days, you'll hardly notice them."

She eyed him judiciously; and he did not say no. Moving on rapidly to other considerations, she questioned him about the provisions she had ordered – had the cheeses arrived? The spices? The flour? And hay? What about the dried fruit? And would the abbey's own stores of salt suffice?

"Lady Bonvallet" – John spoke quietly and courteously but, she saw with clarity, through gritted teeth – "you will have to enquire of my cellarer. I have made no inventory of our cheese. May I invite you to step along to the checker and confer with Brother Cormac? I am sure he can furnish you with all the information you need."

The abbot noted that he was shaking with simple anger as he bowed in farewell and opened the door for her to sweep through. He paused and closed his eyes, slowed his breath. Then he turned to the task of preparing tomorrow's Chapter.

Sitting at his desk, he opened the Rule and looked blankly at the passage set. He tried to scrape up from the scattered debris of his excoriated soul something worth saying. He wondered if he could simply pass the responsibility across to Bishop Eric. *Wider and deeper? Richer? More inspiring? Fine. You do it.*

He picked up his pen, dipped it in the ink, drew to him a torn scrap of vellum for making notes. Parchment was valuable, not to be wasted. He hesitated, searching for thoughts worth writing down. *As I sat in my atelier...* No. *As I looked out on the sunrise this fine May morning...* No. *As we prepare to receive a considerable invasion – oh, for the love of God, who's that now?*

He shoved back his chair in irritation and crossed the room in three livid paces, snatching open the door. And there stood William.

"Oh. Not a good moment? I won't come in. But can I just ask you – is it the case that you gave permission for these minstrels the Bonvallets have engaged to impose on your hospitality three days? Yes? John, tell me you said the family will have to foot the expenses. The drain on your coffers from this masquerade is growing like mushrooms on horse dung! She's a conniving and opportunistic shrew, that woman, and –"

"Go away," said John quietly. "Just for now. I am grateful for your help. I appreciate your advice. But just for the moment – please – give me some space. Yes, I gave my permission. Please go away. Just for now. Please."

He tried to smile, but failed. He had to trust William to understand as he quietly closed the door again, right in his face.

Once more he stopped, applied himself to restoring calm and concentration; then the bell began to ring for the noon office.

Doggedly, he returned to his work after the midday meal, having directed his prior to find the bishop something to do, and tracked down William to apologize for his earlier discourtesy. But he could not settle, could not think. Scattered like feathers, like blown leaves, his thoughts whirled empty and random. He thought he might as well find Francis and the bishop and at least make himself useful there. He opened the door to the abbey court, but couldn't bring himself to go.

It was then, as he stood in the doorway of his house, within the shadow of its frame, that he saw Brother Conradus crossing the court towards him with a short, comfortably proportioned woman who simply had to be his mother. Deep in happy conversation, Brother Conradus gesticulating and laughing, pausing to point out the checker as they passed it, the door to the refectory, the windows of the library above – they made slow progress. And then she broke off to walk across, over to the wall beneath the refectory windows where a mass of bluebells, fading now but still in bloom, gave out such a glorious fragrance. And John watched her kneel unselfconsciously and unaffectedly, putting out her hands to the flowers, bending her face to them, breathing in the perfume. Brother Conradus came to stand beside her, and she turned her head, lifting her face, her smile full of delight and appreciation. *That's where he gets it from, then,* thought John. *I wish more of your sons had vocations, Rose. We could do with the whole tribe up here.*

She held out her hand and Conradus pulled her to her feet and into his arms for a quick hug, then they continued their cheerful, sauntering transit along the path bordering the west range, to the abbot's house. Eventually Conradus saw his abbot standing in the doorway and evidently said as much to his mother, for they both looked his way, Conradus with a cheery wave, and quickened their pace.

As John stepped back in to admit them, Rose held out both her hands to him, much as she had to the flowers, and her eyes searched his face with keen perspicacity; something sharper and deeper than the usual glance of first acquaintance, something seriously appraising but as kind and gentle and happy as it was wise.

After his initial greeting, John asked her, "Will you be weary now? Shall you first rest?"

She hesitated. "I've ridden far," she said, "but I am eager, too –"

"To hear about the wedding?" John anticipated. "Is that best?"

Rose smiled. "Oh yes – but more, to spend some time with you. Our lad writes home about his Abbot John, in every single letter that he sends."

"Aye, Rose – we likewise know you through your son; I almost feel that we're already friends."

She nodded. "Then may I – but I don't want to impose. If I would be a nuisance, you must say –"

"Ah, no! You are most welcome; truly, Rose. I've been so looking forward to this day." John thought he could make as much time for this woman as she wanted. Her face lit in the brightest smile, and she confessed with honesty as limpid as a child's: "It's such a big adventure to come here!"

John laughed. "You're welcome, with wide open arms, my dear."

Brother Conradus, observing this first encounter of two of his favourite people with pleased satisfaction, felt it couldn't have been better. "I told you," he said, "you'd absolutely love her!"

Rose turned to him, her eyebrows rising and her eyes wide, "You told him *what*, lad?"

"Oh," he said, "you can say anything to Father John. Besides, it's true; look."

"Well," said John, "sit you down, both of you. Oh, but Rose – forgive me, rude – this is Brother Thomas, who looks after me and keeps me in order. One or other of us is usually here if you're looking for me."

Having greeted her, Tom offered to go with Conradus to the kitchens and fetch some refreshment for Rose after her journey. He closed the door to the abbey court, and the two men went by way of the cloister.

"Your husband has not come with you?" John asked, both of them choosing, without really thinking about it, to sit not on the chairs for important guests but on the two low stools.

"Oh, no. The garden, the animals – I mean, we have one lass still at home with us – our Alice – and the others are nearby, they'll always help out, but this is too many days. Though Father Chad did invite him, and Gavin thought maybe he'd ride up for the wedding, so then I could go home with him afterwards – save one of the brothers turning out a second time. Jane – our Simon's wife – will stay with Alice while her dad's away."

"You take good care of each other," observed John.

"We – aye, I suppose we do. I expect our Alice could manage alone, but she might feel a bit forlorn all by herself with her dad and me off on a jaunt having a wild time. I'd be sad to think of her lonely."

"Conradus is the same," John said. "It's not so very long since I had the most awful family tragedy myself. My mother and sister… some unspeakable louts set their house afire, killed my mother. My sister… they… a whole gang of them… they… hurt her. It tore me apart, and for a while I was good for nothing. And your lad was so gentle to me, and so very kind."

Rose listened to this, still and serious. "I am so sorry," she said. "I hardly know what to say. Your sister? How is she now?"

"Oh…" John hesitated.

"I don't mean to be nosy," she said quickly.

"No, it's all right. She lived here with us for a while, but now she lives ten miles hence. She married. I believe she is well enough settled. You'll meet her husband. He's also here to help with this wedding. He's called William. He… well… perhaps I'd better leave it there. He's a dependable man; I can trust him to look after Madeleine. But it's the same as with you – she couldn't come with him because they have chickens and geese, a goat and a garden. They used to keep pigs, but not now I believe."

And so they talked easily about homely, family things, and the life Rose sketched out for John reminded him of his childhood, the way he grew up. He felt comfortable with her, his eyes resting on the soft contours of her face, rosy cheeks, dark eyes, dark hair streaked through with silver like his sister's, stray wisps of it escaping from the linen cap she wore and curling softly against her neck. Her hands, plump like the rest of her, brown from the sun and very clean, rested peacefully in her lap as she chatted. She dressed modestly, he noted – her cap, her kerchief folded over her breast and taken round to tie behind her – and he liked that. She had, he thought, an odd combination of quietness and vivacity, so that her presence felt calm but sparkled with the same inherent joy and zest for life as he felt in her son. He found himself telling her things that normally felt insignificant, too inconsequential to say; and she listened, her eyes alive with interest, her mouth almost curving in a smile always ready.

When Tom and Conradus returned from the kitchen, she tasted appreciatively the soft honey cakes and crisp little pastries her son set before her with pride, and gratefully sipped the camomile tea Brother Tom poured her. She listened carefully as they explained what was needed of her in helping with the wedding preparations, and that for this short time she would by special permission be allowed to work within the cloister. She thought about this. "That is a privilege indeed," she said, "and to work alongside my son again is a precious gift I had not looked for. But… the only thing… sometimes, Father John, when I'm cooking – I just can't help it – I do start to sing. Because I feel happy. But maybe that would be out of keeping here. Unseemly. Only I think it might just happen. Even within the cloister."

She looked up, concerned, into his laughing eyes. "Oh, Rose, thank God you've come!" he said. Somehow, everything about her set the bishop and the Bonvallets and the whole struggling endeavour of trying to live up to the status of the abbacy into better perspective. It unaccountably faded away. They'd only just met, but he felt as though he'd known her forever.

Chapter Three

They walked through the apple orchard, the trees laden with pink and white blossom, to the infirmary, where Rose especially wanted to see the physic garden. As they strolled along, they talked about healing herbs, and Rose's knowledge delighted John. Some of what came out in their conversation was familiar to him already – lettuce as a sovereign remedy for heartburn, the dangling flowers of the nettle as a wonderful spring tonic – but other snippets about winter aconite for tumours and flowers of hawthorn to strengthen the heart, were new to him. She surveyed the beautifully tended knot-garden full of the infirmary's medicinal plants, her eyes bright with pleasure. She walked among the herbs, bending to touch and to sniff the clean, robust bouquet of aromatic scents.

Rose thought her son had it right – you really could tell this man anything. His manner was so understanding, so warm and kind. Besides, she felt so free and at peace in his company – a man of God, vowed to the monastic way of simplicity and holiness. She felt less cautious and guarded than she would ordinarily be with a man. Even now in middle life, her hair turning grey and her waist expanding, she took care to exercise the discreet reserve of propriety in her dealings with men. But, believing in him, in his vocation, with John she felt at liberty to simply let him see who she really was, and share with him the interior landscape of her soul. She trusted herself to him.

As they walked back to the checker, they talked of the care of the sick and dying, of human nature and the threads of faith, the bright thread of love and courage – gold, she said; red, thought John – and the thread of peace – blue, said John; green, said Rose – woven into the stuff of everyday life; strengthening and stabilizing it.

In the checker, he introduced her to Brother Cormac, showed her where to find information if she needed it, where the keys of the storerooms and cellars hung. From there he took her to the refectory, to show her the quickest way into the kitchen from the guesthouse.

Father Theodore, who had left most of his novices working on their New Testament Greek, dashed down to beg his abbot's attendance at the bishop's second visit to the novitiate. He didn't know when that would be, but assumed it must be soon, since the Visitation was generally accomplished in three days; so he thought he'd ask now.

He had been greeted at the cloister door to the abbot's house by Brother Tom, who said the abbot would most likely be in the vicinity of the checker. With a hastily suppressed sigh of exasperation – he ought to be overseeing his charges – Theo strode across the atelier, opening the further door in time to see John and Rose walk across the greensward from the checker to the refectory. He stopped in his tracks, watching John's eyes crinkle in a spontaneous moment of genuine, unaffected laughter, seeing how the abbot bent his head to attend to what Rose was saying, observing the openness, the happiness of her countenance, so lively and natural.

"Oh, no," he said under his breath. "Oh, no, no, no. Oh, sweet mother of God. That's all we need."

Tom came to stand behind, looking over his shoulder. "Don't say it," he said. "Don't say anything. Not to me, not to anyone. Let's hope he'll come to his senses and it'll just sort itself out.

He's canny, is John. Most of the time, anyway. Well…" The two men watched the approach of their abbot and his guest. "At least, he usually is. Oh, he'll catch up with himself."

Theo shook his head in unbelieving despondency. "Quite possibly. But when? After how much damage is done? We're in the middle of a bishop's Visitation, for heaven's sake."

"Theo! Let it alone. I'll have a word with him if need be. Oh look – there's the equerry. I wonder where he's going?"

As John and Rose walked along to the abbot's house Brainard, having discovered Brother Conradus's genius, headed this lovely May morning towards the kitchen. Not only had he a considerable list of his own morsels of choice, but carried in his head Bishop Eric's aspirations for the gastronomic aspects of his stay.

His path from the guesthouse crossed the abbey court, then took him through the refectory into the cloister – the simplest route to the kitchen.

In the refectory, he found Brother Richard and Brother Placidus, hard at work on the dining tables. Richard scrubbed these thoroughly every afternoon, but they wanted waxing to make a nice finish for the forthcoming marriage celebrations. Located in the west range with a door into the abbey court, the refectory offered a convenient space for larger parties of visitors than the guesthouse could accommodate. This didn't happen often – the triduum of Easter was usually the only time of year St Alcuin's received a really sizeable influx – but on this occasion every nook they could think of would be pressed into use; and had to be cleaned first.

Today, Richard had scrubbed the tables down as usual, swept the floors, and had now started on the laborious job of rubbing in the polish. Brother Walafrid made good-sized pots of this, using their own beeswax fragranced with lavender from the garden. The turpentine he added softened it somewhat, and Brother Conradus had set the pot to stand near the kitchen fire since first lighting it this morning. But the consistency remained stiff; applying it to all six tables took some muscle. When the last one had been completed, the first should be ready for the patient work of buffing with first one cloth, then another of softer fabric, and finally with a square of sheepskin – the fleecy side, obviously. Nobody looked forward to this job, but at least Placidus could console himself it had got him out of a long morning of New Testament Greek. Father Theodore had with reluctance given his permission.

Humming a cheery (but sacred) melody, Brainard came into the refectory, and paused to inhale deeply the aromatic mixture scenting the room.

"Ahhh!" he exclaimed appreciatively. Brother Placidus continued his work without pausing; as a novice he was not supposed to get into conversation with the abbey's guests, unless that proved unavoidable. Brother Richard looked up and smiled.

"Good morrow," he said pleasantly.

"Aha!" Brainard contemplated the fraterer with approval. "Now, that's what I like to see – a smiling face. Did you know, Brother... er... smiling while you work makes you more productive? Smiling men get more done! Imagine that! Ooh – look – Brother Er; you missed a bit! Just here; can you see? If you tilt your head sideways – lean to the left a little way – you have to look at it so the light just catches the surface. No, not there – a little further along; by that knot in the wood. Yes, that's right. Ooh, and look – another little patch near the end; only small, but I'm sure you want to do a good job. Oh and another – hahaha! Isn't it a merry thing, how once you really start to look, you see little places missed everywhere! That's right. Oh – another little spot; here, look." He pointed. "How remarkably felicitous I happened to come by. Just think, you might never have noticed. Such occasions – not coincidences to my mind, I like to call them Godincidences – the mini-miracles that blossom unheeded along our daily path. Ooh – another spot here, Brother – er..."

He watched with lively attention as Richard, having little choice in the matter, doggedly persevered with his application of beeswax, baring his teeth in his best approximation of a smile.

"Zounds! Fie! Is that – wait! Just a minute! Go to! There's a mouse!" This elicited little astonishment from Richard or Placidus; the frater hosted plenty of mice. They had a cat, and it hunted valiantly, keeping the population within tolerable limits. But Brainard, moving more swiftly, and more silently, than Richard would have judged within most men's capability, managed to arrest the little creature's escape by treading on its tail. He stamped on it with his other foot, grinding in a vigorous circle to be sure it was dead. Placidus, straightening up from his work, watched open-mouthed. "I think that's done for it – well, nearly; it won't last long," said the jocund equerry. "A bit of a mess, I'm afraid, but nothing a scrubbing brush won't shift. Well, I must be getting on – I've a list of requests as long as your arm for Brother – er – the kitchener." He stepped sprightly towards the cloister door, leaving a faint trail of blood mixed with tiny traces of gut, fur and body fluids in his wake. "Don't forget, now!" Almost coquettishly he looked back: "Keep smiling!"

Brother Richard had always maintained that Brother Cormac, during his days as kitchener, ought not to pepper his speech so freely with expletives, exposing the novices who worked alongside him to an example falling far short of the monastic ideal. But in that moment Richard descended to the same unworthy laxity himself. Realizing that not only had his vocabulary been reprehensibly unrestrained for the presence of a novice, but also the choice opinions he had expressed about a guest of the abbey and the right-hand man of their Bishop Visitor, Richard knew he would have to confess this in Chapter the next morning. It occurred to him that Bishop Eric would most likely be present at the Chapter meeting, and wondered if he ought to say nothing, that being the case. Or go to his abbot and make a private confession – though when he saw Father John earlier this morning, he had every appearance of being wholly taken up with Brother Conradus's mother.

"Well? Is it dead?" he snapped at Brother Placidus, who had gone across to look.

"I surely hope so," said the lad. He sounded upset. "I know they're vermin, but... every creature that lives should have the chance of a gentle death. That's what Father Theo says, anyhow. I'll get the scrubbing brush and a pail of water, shall I, Brother Richard? Clear it up?"

The fraterer nodded, and took a deep breath. "Aye. Good lad. Then we must get cracking with this – it can't be far off time for the midday office. We ought to be laying up in here before too long."

It might have been awkward if LePrique had come upon Rose in the monastery kitchen. No doubt he would have mentioned his surprise in conversation with his master, and feminine infiltration of the cloister was unquestionably undesirable. Bishop Eric, like Father Theodore, would probably have considered it unthinkable. And the kitchener's chances of getting his feast together without her would have been surpassing slim.

Happy it was, then, that having introduced her to his novice master and cheerfully agreed to make himself available for the next examination of the novitiate, Abbot John found so much in common with Conradus's mother, and such a lot to talk about, that LePrique had just gone on his way by the time she hurried along to the kitchen. The equerry left behind an extensive outline of menu suggestions. Conradus actually physically stopped, when his mother walked in, to achieve the conscious accomplishment of changing the expression on his face.

"Good morrow, my sweet ma!" He took the scroll of dietary aspirations and put it rather emphatically on the spike. "Have you slept well? And breakfasted? And do you feel inclined to have a go at some gingerbread? I'll show you my design for the main course subtlety. I drew it up last night. It's going to be awesome!"

✠   ✠   ✠

Father Theodore, out of breath from scaling the stairs at speed, found his novices studying with exemplary quietness on his return. Too quiet, in Brother Robert's case – head resting comfortably on his folded arms upon the desk under the window, he had fallen asleep over his New Testament. The irresistible drowsiness brought on by difficult texts could be palpably felt among them all. So the novice master invited them to regroup into their circle. The physical movement involved in setting out the benches brought them back to life.

"So." Once they had gathered, Father Theodore looked round at their faces. More than one of them thought he seemed a bit flinty today. More forbidding than usual. "Why do we have a Rule?"

His gaze went from one to the other, his eyebrows raised in enquiry. Theodore encouraged question and comment, he took all of them seriously. They knew that nothing they could say as an honest opinion would draw censure or derision from their novice master. This gave them the necessary confidence to explore possibilities without needing to feel afraid of looking stupid.

Anxious to please, seeing Theo looked a little grim, Brother Boniface said: "The other day in Chapter, we had that reading from near the beginning – the one about Jesus' story of the time of storm when the house doesn't fall, because it's been built on the rock. I don't think the rock is the Rule. And I don't think the Rule is doing the building. Because the story in the Bible says the man who listens to the words of Jesus and acts on them is like someone building on the rock – and that's anyone, not just Benedictines. Perhaps not even only monks or nuns. But I think the Rule might be to guide us in that way. Like a builder's apprenticeship, or something."

Theo nodded. He rarely said "Good", or "Right" or "Wrong". He respected their insights and opinions, and let the discussion between them hunt down truth.

"What about the Chapter based on Psalm 119 we had a day or two ago?" suggested Brother Benedict. "About running in the way of God's commandments? The one that said about the monastery being like a school that trains us, our whole life long. To persevere, and be made fit to be in the presence of Christ. I mean – by his grace, of course, too. As well as the Rule."

Theo listened to this thoughtfully. And Brother Cassian said: "I guess everything we need for our salvation is already ours in Christ. The word of the Scriptures and the teaching of Holy Church, and really living those things as we come to understand them. But our Rule... well... I'm thinking, Father, if you come at it from the other side, considering how we'd get along without it. Might it be that with no Rule we'd be unruly? Hit and miss, muddling along, misled by our own preferences and temperaments and inclinations. Taken in by understandable human desires. Like the story you told us about the gardener, whose friend admired his beautiful orderly plot, going into raptures about the hand of the Almighty in the work of creation. And the gardener said, 'Yes, but you should have seen it when the Almighty had it all to himself.' I think the life and growth and beauty comes from the hand of God, but the Rule keeps it tidy and fruitful, so there's something to eat as well as something glorious to look at."

"Just so," said Father Theodore, "but please don't repeat that story in the hearing of the bishop. Though it makes a point, it's not the zenith of scholarly theology. But, yes. Bringing our God-given human nature into a fruitful discipline. Because, thinking about human beings for the moment, not gardens, someone usually gets hurt in short order in the lives of people who act on impulse, who abandon wise discipline, who do what they want because it feels so attractive and they can't see the harm in it. And then comes the reckoning. Later. Tears and trouble and broken friendships, people angry and hurt. The reason we have a Rule, to my mind – though the insights you've offered are just as valid as mine – is because it tends towards peace. By that, I don't mean it's easy, or that it encourages complacency. It doesn't make us idle, or dull. Living by our Rule isn't boring or narrow. But it works for peace in human community. And anyone who has tried to live for five minutes without peace must surely grasp how precious that is."

He paused. None of the lads who sat in the circle listening to him could help but notice the vehemence with which he spoke. Brother Cassian, hearing it, frowned. It sounded as though something might have gone wrong, in that mysterious society of professed brothers, still closed to the novitiate.

"Because peace is so inestimable a treasure," said the novice master, "it follows, as you might expect, that it is not bought cheap. Our life, our Rule – this is a costly way. It costs us everything. It is our calling, our pearl without price. Don't be tempted, brothers, to trade it in. So long as this is your true calling, you won't find anything better. That would be impossible. Brother Robert, are you listening? Because you need to know this. All of us do, from the newest among our novices clear through to the abbot."

✠   ✠   ✠

After Chapter the following morning, John came into the kitchen looking for Rose. He had seen her yesterday – they had walked by the river in the evening, talking about this and that, inconsequential things, the small, dear, bright, ordinary grains and fragments that made up their respective worlds. But he felt it somehow important he should call by again today, just to check all was well. No doubt Conradus could take care of her competently, but John convinced himself he owed her this courtesy, as his guest. He would have liked to invite her to eat with him in the evenings, but – try as he might – he could not imagine her in the same social space as Bishop Eric. She belonged to a different part of him, the life that had formed and shaped him before he came here, or at least before he was elected abbot with all the unwelcome carapace of consequence and responsibility that came along with it. An unacknowledged inside place felt guilty and defensive as he walked along to the kitchen; but he went anyway.

As he stepped through the open door, the first sight to meet him was Rose carefully pouring melted butter onto the surface of multitudinous pots of paté. A shaft of sunlight lit the place where she worked. John stood quite still, watching her, the friendly curves of her face and body, the soft colours of her linen dress and apron, the tendrils of silvering hair that would not stay put under her graceful linen cap.

"Well met, Father! We're getting on fine now, as you can see!" Conradus, cheerful, appeared at his elbow. "Mother's just putting the last touches to the potted meats – juniper berries and bay leaves to go on the top, then they're all done. I've cleared a shelf in the dairy to store them where it's cool. Today we'll start on the cheeses, and by some kind of cunning wizardry I must summon up a place to store those too. The wine is all in place, and the casks of ale. The sweets are done, for the most part. The birds are hanging out back, and we'll pluck them later today. The butter comes after that, and the subtleties. The bread will be the last thing we can prepare ahead of time."

Wiping her hands on a cloth, Rose came to greet him, her rosy cheeks dimpling in smiles. "Wes hal, Father John. I mustn't stop – I've to garnish these little pots before the butter sets hard. But it's good to see you."

"Oh – I can finish those off, Mother! You take a little break. Better still – maybe gather me the salad leaves to send along to the guesthouse?"

John went out with her, into the kitchen garden, each carrying a basket, and they walked along its immaculately tended rows.

"Thank you for helping us," he said to her. "You're making all the difference. Conradus was beginning to look just a teeny bit harassed before you came."

Merry and warm, her eyes laughed up at him. "Aye, I can believe it! There's a lot to get through. But we're equal to it. You know, Father John," she said, reaching out to pluck from the pole beans a leaf where blackfly had begun to gather, "I was thinking only this morning, what is it spurs me on – gives me strength for each day?" She looked up at him, squinting against the sun. He was listening. "And I think I put my finger on it. It first began as a game with myself, when I was just a young lass. I started to see if I could make people happy. I told myself that would be a kind of magic." She smiled. "Better not let the bishop hear me say that, eh? But I think my secret's safe with you! It turned into a habit, something I almost – not quite – stopped thinking about. When I see anyone looking sullen or feeling low, I watch them, think about what they enjoy, ask myself what might have gone adrift. And then I see if I can't do some small thing to brighten them up. I'm not a rich woman, Father John, as well you know. I'm not important or clever. I learned to read, after a fashion – well enough to know the words in a recipe, but nothing like the Latin and so forth that our lad's learning here with you. But I – well, I'm nobody and nothing really. And I'm not beautiful. That's a kind of confession. All women want to be beautiful, Father John, and I know I'm not."

Oh, Rose, yes you are, he thought; but he didn't say it. He just listened.

"But it came to me, making people happy is so great a power, so beautiful a thing, that if I could do that, it would make me…

well…" She hung her head, blushing to admit this private thing. "I thought it would make me like a queen." She stood quiet for a moment, then she said, "So that's what I do. Every day. It brings me joy, and that joy is my strength. Magic. Power. Making people happy."

She risked a shy glance at him, to see how this glimpse into her private world had been received, and saw understanding in his eyes, and tenderness. "I think you know what I mean," she said. "I think maybe you do it too."

He began breathing again. "Well, I will now," he said. "Always, I do believe. Thank you, Rose."

"Oh! It's only a little thing, but it does make a difference. It doesn't take a lot to make people happy, I find. To be considered and remembered, comforted and fed. Just ordinary things. Asking how the day went, bringing them a drink. But now – hark at me, prattling on while our lad's put to it to get all done back there in the kitchen! Here are we idling in the garden together – let's get him the greens that he asked for."

As John went along the row, doing as his mother had taught him in his boyhood, plucking out some leaves and leaving some to grow on and renew the plant for further harvest, a memory obtruded into his mind of William and Madeleine in her garden during her time at the abbey – and how he had said to William, crisply: "One word – boundaries!" But this, as he told himself, was obviously different. For he was the abbot, and owed Rose the courtesy due to a guest. He wondered vaguely where the bishop was, and decided not to care. His world seemed to have drawn apart into contrasts of light and shadow; these vivid moments of satisfying, delightful conversation sparkled like sunlight at noon. They send into dark, recessive hollows of meaningless tedium the round of the day shaped by bells and chant and silence, the duties of administration, the obligation of courteous attendance upon Bishop Eric. And the Bonvallet family simply grated on his nerves; he stopped trying to pretend to himself that they didn't.

He made himself leave Rose in the summer garden, willed his feet to take him along the cloister to his house. In the rest of the day, he listened politely, he spoke with as much intelligence as he could muster, he tried to put his mind to the never-ending pile of documents accumulated on his desk. But his heart was not there. Then, halfway through the afternoon he remembered he'd promised the bishop over lunch to show him the library. It must be nearly time for None, but he thought he'd better take a look, in case his Lordship had gone straight there instead of coming to find him first.

As the abbot came out of his house, something caught his attention. Obviously he could see monks in the cloister at most times of day; it wasn't that. What made him look twice was the absolute dejection in the young man's demeanour; Brother Robert mooching dismally along the cloister as if he'd lost interest in arriving anywhere. John felt it more than sure he would already be keeping Bishop Eric waiting in the library, so he considered leaving Robert to sort his own problems out. But he reminded himself of the priorities of Jesus, which didn't rank status and position as a more compelling imperative than the struggles of ordinary people, and he strode briskly after Brother Robert to find out what had gone wrong.

Not a gifted man, Robert had no expectations of setting the theological circles of Christendom alight with his insights any time soon. His illumination work was frankly awful, and though his lettering stood up tolerably well his spelling hampered him. Not quick-witted, he often missed the point of the understated jests, the puns and parodied references, characterizing the conversation of the novitiate's leisurely moments. His departure from the world into monastic life had left no trail of broken hearts; in fact, though he had three sisters and two younger brothers, it would be accurate to say no one missed him much at all. Here in the abbey, he worked alongside Brother Thaddeus in the pottery. Their craftsmanship directed itself towards the production of simple, serviceable vessels for everyday use, and under Thaddeus's kindly tutelage Robert had begun to shape up into first a passable craftsman and then a good one.

Seeing time was short because he wanted to be on his way, John felt relieved that it usually required no oblique diplomacy to draw Brother Robert out: a straight question would do. And so it proved today.

Father Gilbert, he explained, had co-opted the entire novitiate to sing the polyphonic setting of the Mass for the forthcoming nuptials. Several of the young men had fine voices, as did Father Theodore. Mostly just two or three of them were required to learn new solos for acting as cantor as their turn came round; but this music was difficult and asked for a full choir. Father Gilbert needed them all; except, as it turned out, Brother Robert, who came in early however often he was told (late would have mattered less), seemed incapable of following a conductor, and sang flat.

Robert had no aspirations to further the cause of monastic music, to shine or succeed. His company was dull – his fellow human beings had left him in no doubt of that. He lacked the quick sensitivity of insight that makes men loved, the agile wit that draws admiration. Neither did he have the quality of spirit to scale the heights of prayer or undertake the heady adventures of mysticism. Even his voice was boring. Barely even useful, as he knew quite well, his ambitions could hardly be considered lofty. He just wanted to be included, to have other men laugh at his jokes and let him join in. And though in general they tolerated him with good humour, today they had not. Father Gilbert, driven to distraction by Robert's unexpurgated incapacity, had eventually, not exactly mean but with asperity, suggested he could be better occupied in the pottery. So all the others got to work on the Mass setting together, but not him. And he knew that later, in their hour of recreation, the talk would be all of the intriguing challenge of tackling polyphony, all about the Mass on which every one of them except him had been working.

He explained this in his straightforward way. It never occurred to him to turn it to any kind of quip or pretend it didn't matter. He just related it dolefully, and then stood there looking miserable.

John's first reaction to this tale of woe was impatience. The young man's biggest problem seemed to be complete self-absorption. But on the very edge of saying "Oh dear, I'm sorry about that; well, never mind," he pulled himself back.

"Will you be – can you be – firing pots in the next week?" he asked. "Have you anything ready?"

"I'm not sure we'd planned to, but we could," said Brother Robert. "It takes five or six hours to bring the kiln up to full heat after we've built and stacked it, but if we start early it'll be done and cool down in time to unload the next day. We've got some pots made only wanting the addition of slips and glazes. A few big platters and some bowls and drinking cups."

"Well, why," suggested his abbot, "don't you and Brother Thaddeus decorate them with some pictures or lettering suitable for the wedding? Nothing too tricksy. A picture of a man and a woman, or just their names – if you like the idea, I'll write 'Hannah' and 'Gervase' down for you on a wax tablet, and leave it out on the scribe's desk in my room. Then if you can get them fired in time, Brother Conradus could use the platters for fruit or cheese, or pastries, and the cups could take pride of place at the wedding feast. Just an idea. Tell Brother Thaddeus I'd like it done if he can see his way to it."

As he watched Robert's crushing despondency give way to delight, saw the excitement in his step as he hurried off to the pottery, filled with enthusiasm to begin, the abbot reflected that taking the trouble to be kind wasn't all that difficult. Yet its results were transformative. He smiled, enjoying the energetic bustle of Robert vanishing along the cloister. Then he turned away, and made for the library, where he hoped Father Chad had found the inner reserves to keep his Lordship amused.

He paused at the library door, hearing voices within. *This is getting to be a habit*, he thought – *eavesdropping*. Not a practice he admired, but there was something about a Visitation that seemed to develop stealth.

"And this –" he caught the tone of pride and reverence in Father Chad's voice: their showpiece – "is a book of Bishop Aelred's sermons – Bishop Aelred of Rievaulx – written and bound by his own hand!"

Don't tell him that, he'll snitch it for his own place! The abbot noted his own immediate instinct to clutch tighter what he feared might be taken, and thought it did probably not spring directly from the Gospel.

"Really? Let me see." John's heart sank as he heard the avaricious note in the bishop's reply. He heard the sound of stiff vellum pages being turned in the silence. And then: "*Very* interesting. No – leave that out, please. I'll have a word with your abbot about it." *Oh, you idiot, Chad*, thought the said abbot.

"What else have you?" enquired the prelate. "What is your own particular area of study? Who are your favourite theologians?"

John listened for the answer to this, realizing with a sense of surprise that he had no idea what it would be. He wondered what Father Chad liked to read, what he thought about, and felt ashamed that, had the bishop asked him the same question about Chad's reading habits, he would have been at a loss to supply the information. And then he found out why.

"Well…" Now the librarian sounded nervous and apprehensive. "In truth, your Lordship, I am not a great reader. I dust the books and keep them tidy. I take good care of them, checking for mildew and beetles. I make sure everything is in good order. But I don't read much... at all... really."

Though silence is essential to the art of listening at doors, inwardly the abbot groaned. *For pity's sake, Chad! Surely you could have come up with something better than that? Surely you must have read something – even if it was only in the novitiate.*

He thought he heard astonishment in the ensuing hiatus. Then: "For what reason, Father... er ... what did you say your name was?"

"Chad, your Lordship."

"I see. Who, Father Chad, made you librarian?"

"Our present abbot – Father John," came the reply. *Thanks*, thought John.

"Why? If you don't read. Surely a novice could dust the books."

No answer. The air filled with the silence of the bishop waiting. Then: "I used to be the prior." Chad spoke quietly. "But I was unequal to the demands of that obedience. My vocation means everything to me, your Lordship, but I am in no respect an accomplished man." Something in the humility of that honesty hurt John's heart. It could not be easy to live every day with such accurate self-knowledge.

"I am not gifted in pastoral care, and I am no scholar. I am timid, and some of our guests can be... difficult. And... this became important... I do not find it easy to forgive. So I asked Father John if I could be relieved of that heavy obedience. Out of kindness, he required it of me no longer. It exhausted me. And he let me work here, and in the garden – for the peace. For quiet work to nourish my meagre soul."

How strange, thought the abbot, listening. *Knowing your own insufficiency immediately beefs up your spirit – makes you more than you might have been.*

"But you know Latin? You know Greek? You have studied – at least in the past? How are you fulfilling your duty of pursuing the study of your religion?"

"Well… your Lordship… this probably doesn't sound much. Sometimes when Father John speaks to the daily chapter of the Rule, read in the morning meeting, he treats of some word of the Scriptures – something in Latin or Greek. For instance, a while ago he spoke to us about two words – *parvo et humilis*. *Parvo*, he said, means 'small' and *humilis* means 'humble' or 'earthy'. He told us that *humilis* forms the same root for both things – for humility and for humus, the nutritious, peaty earth plants can grow in. He said these qualities are the stuff of the Gospel. That we cannot walk in the way of Christ without them. We must be *parvo* and we must be *humilis*. Lowly, humble, content with insignificance, willing to be of no account. Close to the earth. What he called 'the valley spirit' – the lowliness in which streams may flow. In such earth will root the tree of righteousness. That's what he said. I remembered the Latin words, because how he explained it made sense to me. And Father John's Chapters are short and easy to understand, so I can take it in. But because these books are long and difficult, I find them… abstruse and… boring."

At least he knows the word "abstruse", thought his abbot, but decided the word "boring" would not help things along, and felt the time had come to intervene. He pushed open the door. "Ah! My lord bishop – here you are! Good afternoon, Father Chad. Oh – I see you have been looking at our book of Aelred's sermons. We prize it greatly. It is one of the treasures of our library. Occasionally other foundations ask to borrow it, but we do not lend it out – though we are willing to make a copy from time to time. Did you find any other volumes to take your interest in particular? In my work as an infirmarian I have found our herbals especially useful. Our physic garden was laid out according to the

90

same plan as the one at St Gall, from the book here. And we have some excellent texts – they are in the order of the alphabet – see – Anselm, Augustine, Averroes, Avicenna – some foundational documents for study."

John realized as he gestured towards the shelves that, when it came to it, he didn't know a whole heap more than Father Chad. Neither the infirmary nor the incessant interruptions of the abbacy left him a massive amount of time to lose himself in books, even if he had the inclination. Which Chad's simple honesty reminded him, he did not.

But the bishop inspected, considered, nodded, said little. He looked round for the book of Aelred's sermons once his tour was complete: but Father Chad had already put it away. "Thank you," said his Lordship, "Father – er – Father Chad. That seems satisfactory."

Bishop Eric dined with the abbot, but his conversation that evening focused not so much on the library as on the school, where it transpired he had spent a good part of the morning. *Why didn't I know this?* wondered the abbot. *Where was I this morning?* In the abbey school, the bishop found little to criticize; the children had recited their lessons well. His only reservation – they seemed very happy and confident.

"Boys," he advised, "need keeping under. It is essential they understand authority. They have to know who's in charge. Boys will always take advantage of leniency. Your Brother – er – the novice, the lad who helps out – he should be cultivating an altogether sterner and more distant manner when it comes to the boys. A bit of fear builds their character, keeps them in line. I see there's a birch rod fastened up on the wall, but I ran my finger along it and, Abbot John, the thing was actually dusty! It should be used, and used within sight of the other lads. It should be soaked in brine, you know, for good effect. It's how they learn discipline, how they grow up to be men."

The abbot listened to this, looking into the amber depths of his wine as he swirled it slowly in his pottery beaker. He could think of no appropriately affirmative reply. "Is it?" he asked quietly. The bishop's canny gaze rested on him.

"Things come undone," he said, "in any establishment infected by indulgence. You cannot govern with kindness, Abbot John. You cannot keep order where you pamper the faults and foibles of men and boys. What starts as weakness strengthens into vice. Too much sympathy is the downfall of any régime. A little fear adds spice, holds them up to the mark, keeps them on their toes. It's good for them – for men and boys alike. You will need to make them afraid of you if you are to succeed."

Mater Dei, thought the abbot. *Really?* He kept his eyes meekly lowered, and did not speak.

"Well?" Bishop Eric did not intend to let him off that lightly. "What do you say?"

"Thank you," said John carefully. "I am new in this role, and I have so much to learn. Any guidance is always helpful to me. I know I must have my blind spots. I will look into the school, your Lordship, with your words in mind. I do take very seriously the discipline of my house."

After that, the talk between the two men seemed to run into the dust. The bishop thought he'd take a stroll down by the river before Compline. John knew he was meant to offer to go with him, but couldn't face the idea. At a very deep level of his being, he felt he'd seen enough of him for one day. With all respectful courtesy, he ushered him out and closed the door behind him.

"I'll help you take those dishes through to the kitchen, Tom," he said to his esquire, who had begun to clear the table.

Brother Tom heard this without surprise. In the normal way of things his abbot left him to it; clearing the table was Tom's job, not John's. If a spare half hour between supper and Compline presented itself, he would take it as a chance to work on his

Chapter address for the morning, or catch up with some of the theological reading it was so easy to let slip. But the kitchen had acquired a remarkable attraction in these last few days. *This can only end in tears*, thought Tom. "Bring that gravy jug then, and the flagon of wine?" he said.

The two men found Brother Conradus and Rose wiping down the tables. It was Brother Boniface's turn to serve, but Father Theodore wouldn't let any of his novices help (or eat) in the kitchen while they had a woman working there. Both John and Conradus thought this seemed excessively scrupulous, but Theodore had proved more sticky about Rose's presence than John had ever imagined he might. The abbot, after showing her the checker, the chapel, the infirmary, had been seized by the idea she might like to see the novitiate room where her son had spent so many hours in his formation as a monk. He had asked Theodore when might be a convenient time to bring her; the novice master had looked at him with a face like a stone wall. "Can she come up to meet the novices? No, I think – I don't wish to disappoint you, Father Abbot – but I think perhaps better not." He had seemed unduly guarded in his manner, unusually reserved. Simply shy, perhaps, thought John. Not many women came here, after all. Though he hadn't been shy with Madeleine; he'd been her confessor. And some other of the village women came to Theo to make their confession, too. Seemed unlikely he'd be shy. But he seemed extremely reticent in his manner toward Rose, more than John could really understand.

Rose, used to hard work and unaware of the ripples her presence sent through the whole community, at the end of this long day simply saw what had to be done and helped her son finish off.

"Where would you like me to put these?" the abbot asked humbly, addressing the question to Rose rather than Conradus, since she was nearest him. With cheerful thanks, she took them from him and stowed them away.

"And now," she said, untying her apron, "I'm going to sit out in the garden for a little while, and watch the sun go down."

John smiled at her. "I'll come with you," he said.

"Thanks so much," said Conradus, beaming with affection at his mother. "It's been a busy day. I'll finish off here, and see you in the morning."

Tom set down the dishes he had brought, by the sink. He said nothing. With one quick glance he read the warmth of John's smile, the unaccustomed softness of his abbot's face.

As Conradus began to sort out the butter dishes ready for the next day, and Tom went back to the abbot's house to set everything in order there, John followed Rose out into the garden. They sat on the stone steps looking over the rows of beans, the onions and the salad greens, watching the undersides of the clouds blush pink against the fading azure of the sky.

"A full day?" asked Rose. "Has the bishop kept you busy?"

John laughed. "Yes, indeed. He... I have a lot to learn. We don't always see things the same way."

"Ah, well," said Rose, "each to his own. I can't imagine at all what it must be like to be the abbot of a monastery, but I've been the mother of a large family, and perhaps that gives me a little glimpse, in a way. We each have our own way of doing things. I've found I can learn from my mother, from my sisters – but in the end I have to do things my own way. Maybe it's the same with you? That you could be grateful for the bishop's wisdom, and take his advice to heart, but still be how God made you, be the man God called you to be? You have to have a system, but it has to be your own."

John absorbed these words as he looked out at the green of the plants and the beautiful gold now swelling out from the western rim of the sky.

"I... I'm not entirely sure I have a system, to be truthful," he said. "I can't even account for how I found myself in this position. Sometimes it feels as though I'm just bundling along between birth and death, making the best of it I can, picking up the bits life throws at me and trying to make some sense of them. But they don't always seem to fit into a pattern."

He liked the sound of Rose's laugh. Not loud or immodest, but easy, happy, free.

"I know what you mean!" she said. "It can get frantic, catching whatever's thrown at you and trying to think what to do with it! But… Father John, I hope this is not impertinent of me; it's not for me to advise you, my son's abbot."

"Go on," he said.

"Well then, when things seem tangled and muddled, too fast and too much, I try to imagine our Lord in heaven, looking down and knowing what it all means – where it's going and what it's for. I think of it as if I had to work blind, but he can see. I listen for him saying, 'Pick up this first, Rose; now you need that; now this comes next.' And I trust him to lead me step by step, and that's how I get there."

She sat, her face quiet and thoughtful, her hands folded peacefully in her lap. "There was one time," she said, the memory bringing a smile, "when I had just too much to do. Little children underfoot, a babe at the breast, my man coming home hungry, the bread risen and needing knocking back, the pots still dirty from the last meal, and the garden in parched ground begging for water. I almost despaired. I begged Our Lady to help me, for was she not the mother of a family like me? She would understand. And the thought came to me, *Look for the gold, Rose. Look for the golden thread and weave it in.* I realized that in every moment of every day, there is something that shines. Something the light falls on." She laughed. "I'm sorry, am I talking in mysteries? This isn't easy to explain. What I mean is, even when I feel so beset with tasks undone that I hardly know where to turn, if I stop and look, there is one thing the light shines on – something that really matters. And the gold, it's the royal thread, the holy one. It's love; it's kindness. I mean, if my man has to eat from a dirty dish, well that won't hurt him. If all he has for his supper is a hunk of cheese and an apple, well that's good food. But if I leave the baby crying, and turn a sour face to my man coming home, in favour of washing pots and cooking complicated dishes, I've let the gold thread go, I've picked the wrong thing. The gold thread is the one that reflects the light. It's the one the light shines on. The beautiful thread. Kindness. The loving thing to do."

The last light shone from the west and though the sun had not yet gone down, the shadows began to gather in the hollows. John turned his head to look at Rose. To his consternation, though he did not move, his hands could feel the warmth of her shoulders and the texture of her linen dress, his mouth knew the feel of her cheek as if he had kissed it. The sense of intimacy and immediacy jolted through him like a shock, something more than he could assimilate. He felt the power of it travel through his whole body. The loveliness and gentle wisdom of this woman. He looked away again. In the grass, a forget-me-not, ardent sweet blue, just coming into flower. He wanted to pick it and give it to her. Caught in the confusion between the insistent clamour of warning arisen with him, and the anguished rebellion of his heart, he did not move. He sat as still as a stone.

Resonant upon the dying light, the bell rang out for Compline, calling the community to put the day to rest. Rose stood up, turning to look down at John as he still sat on the step. "Father John?" she said. "Time to go." And so it was.

After Compline, John trod slowly along the cloister to his lodging, his heart full of a turmoil of emotion that he did not wish to explore or recognize. He and Tom had tidied up before chapel, so his esquire did not come back with him to his house. He stood in its silence, alone. And in the quietness came the faintest knocking on the outer door. Frowning in puzzlement, he crossed the room and opened it; and there in the dusk stood William.

"We are in Silence," said the abbot.

William nodded. "I know," he said softly. "I ask your pardon. Even so, of your charity, may I come in? It's only one thing. I won't intrude long."

So John stood back to let him enter, and gestured to the chairs by the cold hearth in the darkening room, where only one light burned, enough for a man in solitude. "Is something wrong?"

"Well... I went this afternoon into the checker. Brother Damian had asked if we could have two of these new hornbooks for the school. Brother Tom made them, they did the lettering upstairs, and they'd just finished them. Brother James brought them down to Cormac for approval today. They did a good job on them, too. Very nice. Nifty things. So I took them across to Brother Damian, to spare Cormac the chore. And he said Bishop Eric had been in earlier in the day, and all had gone well except his Lordship was complaining that the birch rod seemed little used. That no schoolmaster can keep order without making an example of a lad from time to time by means of a good birching. Essential for maintaining discipline, he said. And that Brother Damian should soak the thing in salt water to harden it. Did you hear of this?"

John nodded. "Aye. He said as much to me over supper."

"And what did you answer him?"

John shrugged. "I didn't argue. But I think we have no plans for laying about the lads unless they give us good reason. Besides, salt's expensive, and I should think we have better uses for it than that. Why do you ask?"

He wasn't quite sure how this impression came about, but in the shadows William's eyes seemed almost like lights, so intense was the spirit that illumined his gaze. Not for the first time, John reflected how strange and how considerable was this feral soul.

"In the house where I spent my childhood, we had an upper floor," said William. "Much like your hayloft, where I've spent my nights since Bishop Eric showed up. A store-place, with a wooden ladder stair going up to it from the kitchen. My mother and father had a chamber off the hall downstairs, and I slept up in that loft, among the provisions – the apples and such. Me and one or two rats. It wasn't a big place, just over the kitchen.

"Staying in the loft here has its similarities. Brings back memories, swinging up from the ladder into the store.

"And I remember an evening when I'd gone up as the light went off the day. I'd a straw mattress against the wall, and I lay down there. But I heard my father coming up the ladder. This was never good news, John. It meant I was in trouble. And so it turned out. He erupted through the hatch, raving about something I'd done wrong, or misplaced, or done badly, or forgotten, going on and on. Me on my feet the minute his head came through the hole, or I'd catch it for not showing him due respect. And then he was unbuckling his belt and I had nowhere to run. I went down on my knees, still gabbling excuses and apologies. He grabbed me by my shirt collar, roaring at me to get on my feet, and then he swung his belt for the first slice, buckle end flying – and you cannot brace yourself for the pain. Again and again – oh, Lord Jesus! No refuge from it. I couldn't help but cry out, and I was meant to take it in silence – 'like a man', he'd say, which I wasn't; but sometimes I didn't manage to, which earned worse punishment. I collapsed on the floor and still he was at me, the flying end of it knocking something off the store shelf to the ground with a crash, and that infuriated him further. Lashing me and kicking me, like it would never be over, never end. I wrapped my hands about my head and curled up as tight as I could.

"I've heard say that when someone is set upon, or injured, sometimes they do not feel the pain until later; at the time they are just numb, as though they leave their body in that moment.

It was not so for me. Trapped in my body, trapped in that small room, trapped in that house, in that life, I had no escape and no respite. Do you think it did me good? Kept me in order? Taught me a lesson? It went so deep, that pain and terror and loneliness and shrivelling shame. It cut through all the layers of my body and right into my soul. It disfigured my spirit.

"He had a birch rod, too, my father. He didn't soak it in brine; he wouldn't have wasted good salt on me. If he wanted something harder he just picked up the fire irons, or his belt buckle did a cracking job.

"I went up to the hayloft here, before Compline. I didn't want to go to prayers – my head was full of what Brother Damian had said. He didn't like the bishop's recommendations especially; but he wondered if he'd been a bit lax, letting that birch get so dusty. I just listened to him, left the hornbooks, went away. I couldn't even speak about it, couldn't begin to tell him what it does to a child. Damian – what do I know? No doubt he was thrashed himself, like every lad. I didn't ask. I just wanted to be by myself, when I thought about it. But then, when I climbed the ladder, it brought it all back so vivid. And I had to – you're in silence, I know, and I'm sorry for disturbing you – but I had to say something. Let them… let them have their childhood, John. God knows, there's enough violent men in the world, enough in every passing day to be afraid of. There have been times when I've felt sick with fear – times beyond numbering. Don't … well… tell Brother Damian to go on letting it gather dust. Let them have their childhood, without fear and pain and humiliation. That's all I wanted to say. I'll leave you to your peace."

He got to his feet and gestured John to silence as the abbot began to frame a reply. "It's all right. I don't want to talk about it – I don't want a discussion or an argument. I just wanted to say."

As John stood too, William moved to leave, then hesitated. "The thing is –" he spoke rapidly – "and I'm so ashamed of this, given what I've been and what I've done – I've never forgiven them, John. I hate them. I hate what they did to me. Nothing I could ever put in place made enough of a defence against the memories... more than that... against what I became. It grew right into me. I have no existence separate from it. The terror and the pain, the loneliness... anguish, really. I don't have a separate self that could leave it all behind. It's who I am. I don't know how I could even start to forgive them. I'm so sorry, John. After all you've done for me. But... it changes you, being beaten like that. Don't... here, I mean... just let it stop."

The abbot standing beside him in the deepening dusk listened to this, nodding in affirmation. "Not being able to forgive them sounds entirely understandable," he said quietly, concentrating for the moment on William's childhood rather than the altogether more benign environment of the abbey school. "I hate 'em, too, and I never even met them. But – if you don't mind me asking – when you say you can't forgive them, can I just check? Do you mean you would enjoy to watch them sizzle in the eternal fires of hell? Unquenchable fire – pain that never stopped, agony forever? Would that make things better?"

"Oh, God, no!" William averted his face in disgust. "No. I had a bellyful of suffering and torture. I'm not a good man, but I don't want to visit that on anyone else."

"I see. So then, if you could imagine it was Judgment Day, and your turn came to stand as you are before Christ, would you take the chance, do you think, to tell him exactly what they'd done – ask him to pay them out for what they did to you? Would it be a chance to settle the old score for good and all?"

William shook his head. "No. No. There is so much in my life I'm ashamed of for myself. Whatever they did and were is their own affair. What I am is up to me. I can't imagine any scenario where I'd be standing before Christ and pointing a finger of blame at them. My best hope is, if I fling myself at his feet and plead, he might have mercy on me and let me off my own eternal damnation."

John nodded. "So... if you could choose, you don't want them punished, don't want vengeance? You don't want them roasted and pitchforked, don't want to hear them scream? You don't want the satisfaction of hearing Christ your judge condemn them and send them away to be tortured?"

William frowned. "By heaven, John – what do you think I am? I know I've been a bad lad my whole life long, but don't run away with the idea I sit salivating over other people's pain. I'll give as good as I get if trouble comes looking for me, but that's all. I'm not excited by cruelty."

"But, William – what you've just told me: that's what forgiveness *is*. It's not a sweet tenderness like a warm glow in the heart. It's not saying what was done doesn't matter. It's exactly what you said: the grace to realize that whatever they did and were is their own affair; and you have no desire to visit on them the misery and anguish they inflicted on you. That *is* forgiveness, William. That's what it looks like. Refraining from upholding old scores in the face of Christ our judge. Being willing to accept into your own life the consequences of who you became, for whatever reason. Letting it be between you and Christ, with no one else dragged in. That's what forgiveness means."

Unusually, for him, disconcerted, William stood in silence, assimilating this perspective. "I'll think about that," he said cautiously. "I'm sorry – I said I wouldn't intrude on your time in silence, and I have. I'll go now – right now – and leave you in peace." And he did. He went out into the bat-flitting twilight, latching the door quietly behind him.

Peace? thought John. In the solitude, in the quietness, swirled the impossibly vivid blend of images. The bishop running a finger along the dust gathered on the birch rod. The petal-soft curve of Rose's cheek and the intensity of longing it brought. The frightened boy trying unsuccessfully not to cry out, caught up in a tornado of violence. *Peace? Oh, holy Jesus...* He shut

101

his eyes – that was no good – opened them. Spread his hands involuntarily towards the invisible presence of Christ – to give it all to something good that might bring healing, to reach for some kind of equilibrium in the turmoil of human reality. *Peace?* As if.

He sat without moving in the lengthening silence of the night, struggling to still his spirit, until eventually he reached a state of mind that allowed him to go to his bed, to lie sleepless for a while, then finally leave it all behind.

☩   ☩   ☩

The five visits to St Alcuin's Florence Bonvallet had made in the course of the week, Abbot John had dodged and left her to his prior. Mostly he had been required to be with his Bishop Visitor. Some of the time he had been struggling to cram in urgent correspondence and the preparation of homilies and Chapter addresses. Late at night and early in the morning he had been approving, signing off and stamping with his seal the prodigious accumulation of bills associated with the torrent of extra guests into the abbey. But on one occasion he had been guilty of catching sight of Florence as he came out of his house, and simply legging it as fast as he could in the other direction, pretending he hadn't seen her. Today he felt he owed it as much to Father Francis as to the Bonvallets to accept some share of the responsibility himself, and offer her an hour of his time – or better still, half an hour.

Brother Martin told him she had gone to the refectory, to check on the condition of the tables and their cloths, to be sure the frater had no vermin, to determine the placing of those guests of sufficient status to be indoors and seated, to decide where to situate the harpist. She also found herself in two minds about the minstrels; the simplest thing would be to give them a spot outside; let the harpist entertain the people of refinement and substance, and everyone else could enjoy the juggling and acrobatics, the more boisterous music of dubious ballads about wedding nights, and the hurdy-gurdy. On the other hand, even her more elegant guests had a taste to be amused, so she acknowledged the existence of an argument to give them a brief spot in the refectory. She asked the abbot his opinion on the matter, and he won himself the sourest look imaginable by enquiring what Hannah and Gervase's preferences might be. And now she stood, regal and imposing, one hand on her hip and the other thoughtfully rubbing her chin, as her gaze swept the room, missing nothing. John noticed that someone had made a fine job of waxing the tabletops and buffing them to a glossy finish.

"There's a mouse!" observed Lady Bonvallet, in cold disbelief. She looked at him accusingly. Earlier on in this acquaintanceship, the abbot had felt constrained to please her if he could, to offer their best and remedy any faults she detected. By this time, reduced to counting the days and heartily looking forward to the first sunrise of Hannah's married life, he limited his efforts to remaining both patient and civil.

"Aye," he said. "We do have mice. We keep a cat, but she misses some."

"Then get another one," she responded. The abbot's jaw tightened, but he did not reply.

"You know how I want the tables set out? The top table at the far end there, the others flanking the long walls – then the harpist at the bottom, there."

"Aye, I do. I believe you had a word with our fraterer, Brother Richard, on the matter. I'm not your man, really, Lady Bonvallet. It's not I who will be arranging the furniture for your family wedding."

Florence's mouth compressed into a tight, twisted rune of displeasure. The abbot sounded distinctly unco-operative. She fixed him with a frosty look, and drew breath to speak, but the far door – that led most directly to the kitchen – opened, and in walked Rose, cheerful and pleasant.

"Yes?" Florence re-directed her attention to the interruption.

Rose, smiling, curtsied. "Good morrow, your Ladyship. My son told me you were here. We thought the wedding day might be such a press and bustle of people, and since we have some of the sweetmeats ready and two of the subtleties are complete, we wondered if you might like to be the first to have a quick peep." Her eyes sparkled with fun. Though she spoke respectfully, she made the suggestion sound enticing and delightful. She put some of the magic back. Watching Florence's face change, seeing it light with eagerness and interest, John felt ashamed. A lifetime dedicated to the pursuit of prayer and humility had evidently not taught him the sweetness of manner that seemed to come naturally to Rose.

"May I have your permission, Father John," Rose then asked him, "to take Lady Bonvallet through the cloister to the kitchen? I know it is a liberty, not something for every day. But I think it might mean a lot to her."

Florence, who had taken a step forward, it never occurring to her to seek the abbot's permission, paused and looked at him. She read effortlessly the softening of his face, the tenderness with which he regarded Rose and heard her request. She could see that whatever Rose asked, the answer was never going to be "no" from Abbot John. Her eyebrows rose slightly in astonishment. Intrigued, she watched as the whole demeanour of his body changed; the obstinate rigidity of a moment before melted away.

"Conradus is with you?" he ascertained. "Then, yes; certainly."

Making a mental note to get Rose on her side about the mice, Florence followed this interesting and unexpected person into the kitchen to see what they had made. Not much about this wedding so far had made her happy; but she had to admit, the sweetmeats were the daintiest creations imaginable. They let her taste one of each kind, and she had to pronounce them delectable.

The dragon's head was ready, and they showed her how the body would be formed of artfully stacked shortbreads – "But they must be crisp and the butter quite fresh, your Ladyship, so we'll be making them the day after tomorrow."

Brother Conradus, bursting with pride, showed her the subtleties he had made – the chalice and paten on the altar with gilded glory raying at the back; and a crenellated abbey with open doors revealing a host of tiny pastry people. Florence peered closer. "How did you make their eyes?"

"Poppy seeds, my lady," he said with a smile. Then, the question he could contain no longer: "Do… do you like them?"

Lady Florence Bonvallet looked at the short, plump brother with his ruddy cheeks and shining dark eyes (exactly like his mother), anxiously awaiting her verdict; and in spite of herself she couldn't help smiling back. "I do," she said. "I think what you've made is magnificent. The best I've ever seen. It makes me feel better about the whole thing."

As she escorted Florence away from the monastery kitchen, Rose asked her softly: "Forgive me if I am too forward, or if it's a secret, your Ladyship; I'm just dying to know – what will you be wearing?"

As Florence described the embroidered linen lawn of her chemise and kerchief, the sumptuous green silk velvet cotehardie, with pearls and thread of gold adorning the sleeves, then the deep red surcote with the jewelled braid edging, Rose's eyes grew round with delight. "And on your head, my lady? Oh yes, you said – a kerchief in linen lawn over your barbet! Oh, gracious goodness, you will be perfect! A queen! I shall be serving along with my son on the day, so I'll be able to catch a glimpse. Oh, my! So exciting!" She wisely omitted any enquiry about the attire of the bride.

Lady Bonvallet went home happy; curious about the abbot, too – evidently a man not immune to feminine charm, which she hadn't expected.

Chapter Four

Since he was at St Alcuin's, so said the bishop, he might as well take advantage of the proximity of Byland Abbey to pay them a visit too. He'd just take his equerry; his other two manservants could stay here at St Alcuin's seeing they were perfectly comfortable. He'd be away only one night.

Abbot John had to acknowledge a twinge of jealousy that Byland got off so lightly. But then on reflection, he imagined their porter hurrying across the court at Byland to tell the abbot Bishop Eric had arrived unannounced to look into their affairs, and he thought maybe he hadn't so much to be jealous of, after all. Yet he did wonder, with vague despair, how much longer his Lordship planned to extend his stay at St Alcuin's. He wouldn't still be here when the guests arrived for the wedding, surely? They wouldn't have to try juggling the – unfortunate, as it now began to appear – designation of William as steward of the feast, with keeping him out of sight of the bishop? John refused to entertain that notion, thrusting it from him firmly. Bishop Eric would be gone. It would be all right.

His Lordship had featured prominently at the abbot's supper table most evenings since his arrival, and John saw this one night's absence offered a chance to honour some among his guests who wouldn't mix too well with ecclesiastical dignitaries: like Rose.

This could also present an opportunity to go through final details for the wedding – the small things; where the musicians could be accommodated and any conveyances of guests with more ambitious travelling arrangements than straightforward horseback. He imagined the horses could be led up to the top pasture and put out to graze overnight, but that wouldn't happen by itself, and it occurred to him that he might be wise to check Brother Stephen had been apprised of the idea and hadn't planned to move all the sheep into the same field at the same time. And he thought it was time he took an interest in the extent to which the novices would be mingling with guests, if Theodore wouldn't let them help in the kitchen because of Rose. Would they be putting their hands to anything useful at all, or had his novice master got so protective of them as to restrict their involvement to singing some complicated setting for the nuptial Mass?

So he asked Brother Stephen the farm manager, Father Theodore the novice master, Brother Giles the guestmaster, Father Francis the prior, William, Father Gilbert the precentor, and Rose, to dine with him. He wished he might have included Brother Conradus, but saw the impracticality of his kitchener being required both to oversee the hospitality of the abbot's house and be simultaneously the abbot's guest. In the event, it turned out that Hannah and Gervase intended to call on him in the afternoon, so he included them as well. Yes, Hannah might recognize William, but then she'd be unlikely to have anything to do with Bishop Eric.

All of them came to Vespers except Rose. She stayed in the kitchen to finish off community supper preparations for Conradus. Nobody had told him why the novices who usually helped out in the kitchen had been suddenly withdrawn, and monastic obedience restrained him from complaining or enquiring. He did his best, but with the ongoing daily preparations for the wedding, and more guests than usual at the abbot's table, he accepted with relief his mother's offer to set everything in order while he went to the evening office.

Rose heard the brothers beginning to make their way along the cloister to the refectory after the office. She hung up her apron, washed her hands outside in the bowl by the well, and went the long way round by the lavatorium and the storehouses under the dorter in the south range overlooking the river, coming through a gap in the hedge at the corner of the buildings, into the court. Seeing Hannah and Gervase walking along from the west door of the church, with Father Francis, she hastened to join them. Conradus had told her the couple would be among the abbot's guests, and she felt grateful to know she would not be the only woman.

When Brother Thomas opened the door to them, Hannah was happily describing the detail of her wedding gown – blue, with thread of gold laid down on it in intricate patterns – while Rose listened with every appearance of admiration and delight, asking about the posy of flowers Hannah would carry, who would be minding the children, and whether Hannah intended to wear a crown of flowers over her cap and veil.

She managed to find a tactful moment to break away, allowing the abbot to take her hands in welcome. She smiled up into his face, saying what a privilege she felt it to be invited to his table, mentioning that she had just received word her husband Gavin would be free as she had hoped, to help serve at the wedding, then take her home the day after.

"I heard so much about you from our boy, in his letters home, before I came." Her voice, low and melodic, sounded comfortable and gentle as she took the opportunity to express these thoughts that had been on her heart. "He told us you are wonderful, Father John, and I think, having met you, I must surely agree. I am so glad for the chance to spend these days with him, side by side, setting about work we both love and understand. Thank you for taking such good care of him; it is clear he is flourishing here. Thank you for allowing me to come. Thank you for this invitation tonight." Then, gently, she withdrew her hands from his.

But his eyes cherished hers as he looked down at her, and his face relaxed into softness as he listened to these words. "I am so glad you came, Rose," he said simply. "Sit by me tonight."

For propriety, in the social ordering of things, the abbot ought to have invited Gervase Bonvallet to sit at his right and Hannah at his left. Francis, seeing that he sat Rose where Gervase should go, had to think quickly. William thought quicker, and slid into the place where Hannah should have gone – at John's left hand. Francis immediately saw why. If the place had been left vacant, Gervase would have gravitated there, as the brothers of the community courteously stood back in deference to his choice or invitation. Whoever sat at John's left would be treated to a prolonged contemplation upon John's attitude to whoever sat on the abbot's right, should that individual absorb a significant proportion of his attention. If William blocked that place, it increased the chances of someone lower down the table distracting other guests from the sphere of interaction around the abbot. The move made William look presumptuous, but he didn't care too much about that; and the prior gave silent thanks.

So Father Francis smilingly invited Gervase to sit beside William, and himself took the place next to Rose, with Hannah the other side of him. He left the other men to dispose themselves as they saw fit. Theodore (Francis wished he'd make an effort and try not to look quite so long-faced) quietly took the seat beside Hannah. Brother Stephen, glad of some interesting and jolly company, sat next to Gervase. He'd been in conversation with him about farming earlier in the day. Brother Giles the guestmaster sat next to Stephen, and that left the place at the foot of the table to Father Gilbert the precentor – with Theo on his left and Giles on his right.

The abbot said their grace, and Brother Thomas waited upon them in the usual way.

Though the time was much occupied with strategic discussion of forthcoming hospitality arrangements, John also found time to talk to Rose about matters nearer to their hearts.

"Tell me about your family, Rose," he said to her quietly, once the essentials concerning accommodation of guests and their mounts and conveyances had been agreed. She felt honoured that he should turn aside from the necessary planning of important events, to take notice of the insignificant detail of her humble life. *He makes me feel so special*, she thought; *what a kind and considerate man. Gavin will love to meet him.*

So she described her home to him – the small house with its big family tumbling around; the garden rioting with flowers and keeping them in beans and greens, in leeks and onions and garlic. She told him about the bee skeps, how they stood in a quiet corner; about the ferocious rooster and the gentle one, the brown hens and the white goat – "From Switzerland, my husband says, these goats come. But where is that – Switzerland?"

She talked of her children, the ones who were married and those still at home – "And I know I should let them go, Father John; it's natural they should make their way in the world: but how happy it makes me to have them close about me. I love their company."

He listened, his face loving and gentle, drinking in what she told him of simple, ordinary family life; nobody important, nothing arrogant or imposing or weighty, just the threads of kindness and belonging from which peace is woven. He forgot where he was, forgot to pay attention to his other guests, as he listened to her.

Francis sprang into action, managing to captivate Hannah with gently playful chat, teasing her with suggestions of including some goats among her bridesmaids, laughing together about the flowers they might wear – and whether over one ear, around or between their horns, and whether they could be trusted not to eat them at least until Mass had begun. He kept a weather eye on Gervase, thankful that Brother Stephen had him engrossed in evaluation of livestock and the going price of wool.

Theodore sat in silence, his face sober and grave. Courteously he passed the butter or the gravy jug or whatever he saw was needed, but he said nothing. Absolutely nothing.

The repast Conradus had conjured for them, knowing his mother would be among the abbot's guests, went beyond delicious. Appreciation of the tastiness and artistry of the dishes brought to the table occupied attention to some degree, and recaptured Rose into general conversation; but this only went so far. That she had become the polestar of John's particular world became painfully evident. Francis, without turning his head or ceasing to smile, managed to lift his gaze and catch Brother Tom's eye at sufficient length to signal something extra was required. Tom worked on a rough (but serviceable) rule of thumb: when things get awkward, give them so much to drink they notice little and forget most of that. He put this into effect.

Hannah got distinctly flirtatious – and Francis deflected this adroitly and with grace. He was used to it. Nearly every girl who visited St Alcuin's fell for the prior's smile.

Gervase became loud and boastful, enlarging on his plans to outdo his brothers in every possible respect. The insecurities and anxiety he felt about forthcoming ostracism from his social circle slipped into view.

Theodore, having drunk his wine without speaking, put his finger across the beaker top when Brother Thomas offered more, in firm refusal. John didn't notice what anyone gave him, and went on chatting happily to Rose, who sipped her wine appreciatively, her cheeks slightly flushed, lifting her face to thank Brother Tom with a smile when he offered her more (but she shook her head; no). Brother Stephen drank well and, as Gervase grew increasingly tedious in his resentment, began to nod off to sleep. It had been a long day. Nobody knew what was going on in Brother Giles's head, because Father Gilbert waxed so very loquacious Giles never got a chance to say anything. But he heard more than he'd ever wished to know about Mass settings, the correct production of the voice and the challenges of polyphony.

William sat, half-smiling, watchful, quiet. He let Tom fill his cup – once – but forestalled refreshment by not drinking any of the first serving. He allowed his face to display interest, amusement, involvement, as though the body language of his abbot included him in the conversation with Rose; which it did not.

Eventually Father Theodore lifted his head and directed his gaze the length of the table, past Stephen and Gervase to William, who caught his glance, took note of the silent plea, and acknowledged it with an almost imperceptible nod. William laid aside his napkin and rose from the table.

"I am up at first light to make myself useful," he said, "so must bid you goodnight, Father John. I'll come in to Compline, but…"

He stepped away from them towards the door, standing at a little distance, making it evident he expected the abbot to offer him the courtesy of a farewell.

John looked up, surprised, said to Rose: "Of your kindness, excuse me", then left his place and crossed the room to William, who reached out both hands and took him gently by the upper arms. "Thank you for your hospitality," he said clearly and distinctly. "It has been a delight to be at your table in good company, as it always is."

He leaned forward and kissed John on each cheek, saying as he did so, in an undertone one shade above silence, "You cannot afford to fall in love with a married woman in plain view. I'm serious, John. Let it go."

Then with a friendly smile and a sketch of a bow, he took his leave.

John stood transfixed, gazing after him, and when he moved back to his table of guests, his eyes were lowered and his face flushed. Tom guessed accurately what the import of that inaudible murmur must have been, from the expression of complete mortification on his abbot's face, and felt profoundly grateful to William. He had spent the last half hour wondering if this unenviable task was going to end in his own lap.

Conversation around the table ceased. Theodore sat with his head bent. The others looked at the abbot. The cheerful expansiveness of a few moments before had vanished from John's manner.

"Thank you for your company, good people, and my brothers," he said politely, but he sounded distracted and discomfited. He no longer seemed inclined to look anyone in the eye. And then the Compline bell began to ring.

"You are as always welcome to join us for the office." He offered the remark generally. The flush subsided from his face, but still he kept close custody of his eyes, and his manner had become noticeably reserved. His guests arose from the table immediately, Father Francis and Father Theodore first, then the others – Brother Stephen with a dig in the ribs from Brother Giles – and finally Rose; sensing that they had perhaps unwittingly outstayed their welcome.

It was the prior who took care of the farewell courtesies due to Gervase and Hannah, positioning himself so that he physically blocked the space between them and the abbot. Brother Giles tripped on an uneven flagstone in the floor, and the resulting amusement from Brother Stephen and concern from Father Gilbert filled their attention. Rose hesitated, wondering what had happened, and if she should say something or just leave. John stood where he was beside the table, resting his fingertips on the board, his gaze averted; and then he recollected himself and made the effort to smile and come out of himself.

"Rose, I am so glad you came to help us. Brother Conradus is honestly treasured in this house. His gentle and generous spirit is as much valued by us as his wonderful skills in the kitchen. Thank you for taking the time to make the journey here to help him, and for all you have done, and for supping with us tonight. With the wedding right upon us and the bishop back tomorrow, the next few days will be somewhat breathless. In case my time is taken up and our paths cross little, let me say thank you now, for your willingness to come and help us out."

She stepped forward to stand before him, inclining her head modestly, blushing a little. She took his hand in hers.

For a moment, she closed her other hand around his, then released him. Brother Tom, observing this exchange, saw she meant no more than a gracious acknowledgment of his thanks; just a thoroughly pleasant, sweet-natured woman, who probably had every tradesman in her village wound round her little finger, yet somehow without making other women – or her husband – jealous at all. Father Francis lingered at the door to see her out into the abbey court after Hannah and Gervase. The brothers of the community took the other door, into the cloister.

"Should I clear these things away after Compline now, Father?" Tom asked when Francis, leaving, had closed one door and he the other.

"Yes," his abbot responded abruptly. Then he drew breath to speak. "Brother Thomas –" he hesitated, but he made himself look at his esquire.

Tom smiled at him, and the kindness and understanding in his face deepened John's embarrassment even further. "Happens to us all," said Tom, shrugging. "Only human." He laid down on the table the folded towel he had been holding, and turned away toward the cloister door. "Coming?" he asked. Shaking his head in the confusion of this sudden evolution of circumstances, John followed him in silence, and they walked along the shadowed cloister together with the last few men making their way into the chapel. Quietly and without rush, all found their places. The abbot gave the knock and the community rose for Compline.

The blessing and the *Salve Regina* closed the day, after which the community entered the grand silence until the morrow Mass had been said in the morning. Tom followed John the length of the cloister back to the abbot's house.

Without even a glance over his shoulder at his esquire, John strode purposefully across the room to his inner chamber, which he entered, closing the door quietly but firmly behind him. In the privacy of his bedchamber, he unbuckled his belt, stripped himself of his clothes, and knelt naked on the stone floor, reaching under the bed for the scourge that lay there, as a scourge lay beneath every bed in every cell. Grasping it in his right hand, John laid about his back, chastising himself savagely, until he felt so unbearably sore and bruised that he had no room for any other preoccupation in even the smallest corner of his soul.

In the main hall of the abbot's house, Brother Thomas made sure the fire was safe, stacked the pots, folded and piled the napkins and gathered the knives and spoons. He knew well the sound of a scourge, even through a closed door. He drew his breath in through his teeth, and a little grimace of sympathy clouded his face. "Ow!" he said softly. It took him three trips to the kitchen to clear all away. When he had gathered the last few things, he stood listening, briefly. "For mercy's sake stop, man!" he murmured. His face was troubled as he let himself out of the house, and closed the door quietly behind him.

When John finally threw the scourge back under his bed and pushed up from cramped knees to standing he began to tremble uncontrollably from simple physical shock. The room bucked and reeled about him. Shaking, he picked up his undershirt from where he had flung it on the bed, and put it back on. Resolutely, he overcame the reluctance to don his habit again, and let out an involuntary gasp as the weight of its folds pulled down against what he had done to his back. Dizzy and nauseous, he fumbled ineffectually at the blankets, and took a moment to manage actually to pull them back. Then he crept into his bed, and lay face down, rigid, motionless. He had achieved what he set out to do – something he had never attempted before – driving out any possibility of thinking about anything from his mind by reducing his world to an empty, barren wasteland of pain. It was a brutal trick, but said to be effective. John had disapproved it on the occasions when its results had been discovered in fainting men, sent along for him to patch up in the infirmary. He had used the scourge often enough in a regular way, as ordinary penance to subdue his flesh, but not like this before. As night slowly swallowed the long summer twilight, he lay awake, enduring. His soul, that he had unseated and knocked off-centre in his body, pulsed in waves of misery and shame.

"... in plain view..." Oh, God... and he the abbot... He screwed his eyes tight against the memory. But the train of thought had begun, and he saw Rose's face, thoughtful and intelligent, soft and rounded and pretty. So he moved, arching his back, and that set every hammered nerve screaming again, clamouring out all competition to secure his complete attention. "Oh, God, what a path to choose," he whispered as he subsided, trembling. "You ask so much of us."

He stayed with this pattern of retreating again and again out of memory into pain until the brother – Brother Germanus, he thought it was, tonight – came and stood outside his room with the handbell, and the sound battered into his head the necessity to get up for the nocturnal office of Matins. He struggled, trembling and agonized and sick, onto his knees, leaning forward to reach the little clapper of wood that hung from the bedpost, to knock wood on wood when the cacophony of the bell stopped, for the monk outside the door to be sure his abbot had awoken. And so, at two in the morning, began the monastic day.

116

Before the dew had dried on the grass, William had been into the checker, ascertained from Cormac that all final supplies were in place, inventoried and stored in date order, and set off to discover John's preferences for hospitality to the troupe of musicians and the jugglers expected to arrive within the next two days. It had been agreed at supper the night before that William would help Brother Martin clear a space and heft some straw pallets up to the storeroom above the almonry. The minstrels would sleep warm and dry up there – that was all sorted. But though he judged it unlikely the abbot would want to invite them to his table, he thought John should have the final say on that.

He knocked lightly on the door of the abbot's house, and Brother Tom admitted him.

"Father John not here?" William did not sound surprised. With so much going on, Hunt-the-Abbot had become something of a community occupation.

"Well, he is." Tom sounded reticent. "He's in his chamber."

"Really? Why? I do need to speak to him."

Then William slowed down, and looked properly at Brother Tom. "What's the matter? He's not ill? Oh, please – not right now."

"No, he… last night, after Compline, he… well he went a bit mad with his scourge, I think."

William pursed his lips, thinking. Then he came to a decision and strode towards the door of John's chamber.

"Ah! No – William – you can't just –"

But William's light, quick knock had already been applied to the door, and without waiting for an answer he let himself in and closed it behind him. He found John lying face down on his bed, absolutely still.

"Oh, for the sake of all holy, what *have* you done, man?" William knelt down at the bedside and twitched out the scourge from beneath. "What the devil is this? *Look* at it! Was this

117

Columba's? I'll wager it was! Knotted ends to it – and what's this? Thorns! Thorns stuck into the knots? Ah, mother of God, John, these things are evil! They make me sick to my stomach – I hate them! They shouldn't even exist. Look at me, man! Turn your head and look at me!"

John did more than that. Slowly and carefully, his breath catching as the fabric of his undershirt stuck and pulled against the torn skin of his back, he turned and sat up straight on the edge of his bed. He looked steadily at William, his face white and drawn.

"All right, you've made your point. How dare you come in here and tell me what to do?"

But William, the scourge in his hand, his eyes hard as stone, glared back at him.

"You are the abbot of this place, John. The abbot! What you do, they will do. What you are, they will all be. Savage. Hating their flesh that God made. Is that what you want? Cruel. It doesn't stop with what you do to yourself, it extends beyond to what you do to others. A fierce, unreasonable standard that sets the bar higher and higher to some ridiculous height of purity that no one can meet and everybody gets hurt trying to attain. These things are vile. And this one's having a stone tied round it first and then it's going in the river."

Hampered by the excruciation of his back, by the time John had got to his feet to prevent this course of action, William was out of the room and the door shut behind him. Muttering expletives, taking care not to scratch himself on the multiple thorns with their dried blood and little pieces of adherent dried skin, he rolled up the tails of it and thrust the whole thing cautiously down the front of his tunic. He looked at Brother Tom, who stood watching him with some surprise.

"He's in no fit state to think about what I came to ask him," he said. "I'd better sort it out myself. Talk to him. Get some salve

118

from Brother Michael and make him let you put it on him. I'll see you later. Keep the bishop out of here if he comes sniffing round later. I believe he'll be back from Byland in the course of the day. I'm going to get rid of this disgusting thing."

Without giving Brother Thomas a chance to reply, he was gone. Tom weighed up the best approach to the tasks William had left him. He decided to leave John in peace for a brief while, and headed off to the infirmary to beg a pot of salve. He thought it maybe more prudent to leave Brother Michael out of it. He didn't want to answer to his abbot for spreading his private humiliations further than need be. He went quietly into the dispensary and took what he needed from the shelf. But Brother Michael was in the garden when he left, tucking frail old men under woolly blankets in their chairs out in the sunshine.

"Brother Tom – hi, Tom!" Michael stepped across and intercepted him. "I was looking for you. Someone said they saw you on your way over here. Did you want me? If not, I just wanted to know, is all well with our abbot? He sounded so glum this morning in Chapter. Is he all right?"

Tom closed his large fist around the small pot of salve to keep it out of sight, and grimaced expressively. "He's... yes, he's all right. Not the best he's ever been. Probably he'll come and talk it through with you at some point – I believe he usually does. You don't need to worry about him; but pray for him, maybe."

In the busy microcosm of the monastery kitchen, Rose was also turning over in her mind the odd ending to an otherwise happy evening, wondering what had happened, puzzled by the abbot's sudden change in mood. She had been speaking to Hannah in the brief time John left them to bid William farewell, but it did occur to her that perhaps he had quietly communicated some troubling news. She didn't know. She shook it from her. In the next three days, a great deal must be accomplished.

"What shall we work on today, my son?"

Rose smiled at Conradus, her eyes full of kindness and love; but he thought she seemed somehow subdued, even so. "Is all well, Ma?" he asked her.

"Indeed it is. Perhaps I'm missing your father a little. It's a wonderful thing to be here with you, but very unfamiliar to me. I'm used to being at home." She looked at him. "Abbot John, last night…" Then she changed her mind. "He certainly appreciated that splendid supper you made him. Of course, he usually has important people at his table – the lords and ladies, the bishop – as is his duty. It was very special that yesterday he treated us serving folk who are just helping out. He is a thoughtful man, my son. He remembers the ordinary people."

Conradus beamed at her. "He is the best! I'm glad you've had the chance to stay a few days and meet him properly. So now, today – if I make a start on the shortbread, will you begin the sweetmeats? Let me show you where I've put the marzipan, with the dried fruits. It's not too early to candy the violets today; we can't leave everything to the last minute after all. Storing everything where it won't get knocked or damp is the challenge; but I think we can manage."

As Brother Conradus put the final preparations for the marriage feast in hand, so Brother Giles began to marshal his resources in the guesthouse, checking the towels for any signs of moth or mildew, making up beds, fetching across extra firewood, for the evenings still came in chilly. He asked for – and got – help from the novitiate in the form of two strapping lads to get extra benches out of store. The bishop was expected back later in the day, so the novice master wanted all his novices with him in the afternoon, in case of a final invasion. Meanwhile, as Brother Robert and Brother Boniface descended the day stairs on their way to help out in the guesthouse, their abbot passed them on his way up, greeting them with the barest nod. They agreed he looked distinctly peaky; worn out by ecclesiastical inquisition, was their mutual diagnosis. He looked all in; pale, moving stiffly and slowly, as he climbed the stairs. Outside the novitiate door he paused, his hand on the handle, irresolute. Then, remembering that his novice master owed him respect if not admiration, he knocked, opened it and entered.

"Father Theodore, I need to speak with you."

When his abbot said this, Theo usually moved quickly to make things possible. Even when it was inconvenient, he created privacy, found his novices occupation elsewhere. But here he stood, a bundle of Mass settings in his hand, about to begin his morning lesson, the young men gathering already in their tutorial circle. He looked at his abbot without speaking, his face expressionless, his manner unresponsive. This had never happened before; they had always been comfortable together. "Can't it wait?" asked Theodore.

John bent his head, and for a moment did not reply. When he looked up again, nothing had changed. Theodore's gaze took in the shadowed eyes, the strain in his abbot's face, read it all clearly. "Brother Cassian!" he said, holding out the scores to the novice. "Of your charity, give these out round the circle, if you will. Keep two sets back for Brother Robert and Brother Boniface – they'll be with us presently."

He turned back to his abbot. "Yes?"

Still John waited and did not speak. Then the abbot sighed. Stand-offs took up more time than community life had to offer.

"You're being really rude, Theo," he said, quietly enough that the young men moving about the room should not hear. "And I am your abbot. And if what's going through your head is, 'Then behave like one,' well, that's what I came to say. I'm very sorry. I've come to my senses. You were right, and I ask your pardon. But being right gives you no leave to treat me with discourtesy. And I'd rather have had privacy to say this."

He shook his head, defeated, gave up on the conversation and quietly left the room. Before he reached the top of the day stairs, he heard the novitiate door latch behind him. "John! Father John!" And turning with slow caution, because every movement set the torn skin of his back yammering, he looked back.

His novice master knelt to make his apology, to beg his abbot's pardon for his discourtesy. John, coming to stand before him, spoke the familiar words of forgiveness, and Theo stood again. In silence. Things still weren't right.

John's eyes, dark and unhappy, searched his. "What?" he said. "Have I broken something forever, Theo? Can't this be put right?"

"We rely on you, John," said Theodore. "You can bend the rules, when compassion can find no other course – and, by all holy, do you not! You can make mistakes – we all can, heaven knows. No one is asking you not to be human, and what would be the point? But with that said, there are some things you just can't do. We rely on you to stand steady in your vocation, have the humility to exercise proper caution, make the way you have chosen your clear and absolute priority. You have let us down, Father. You've let yourself down, too. And we have put our trust in you."

John nodded, feeling shame seep inexorably, relentlessly, into all of him. "I know," he said, "but what can I do to put it right? I can't send her home now – Conradus needs her help, and she'd be so hurt; it would look as though she'd done something wrong, when she has not. Nor have I, if it comes to it – I mean, nothing improper has passed between us. No – I know, I know, Theo! I understand full well, and I have let it go. But what more can I do? The guesthouse is filling up with people and the kitchen there just isn't big enough. Conradus needs her in our kitchen here – it's the only space practically speaking where he can prepare the wedding feast. Let's just get through this next week, Theo, and then the dust can settle and we can start again. Oh, for pity's sake, man – I didn't *mean* to fall in love! And was it so very obvious?"

His novice master regarded him steadily. "Aye. It was."

John nodded. "All right. Thank you. Moving on. This afternoon – Tom tells me you want me up here if Bishop Eric comes into the novitiate again. I'll be here."

The door to the novitiate was cautiously opened, and Brother Benedict put his head out. Theodore turned to respond to him, and his abbot left him to it. Still moving gingerly, he went back down the stairs, his face set bleak and enduring. He thought he probably ought to go across to the checker and find out how William and Cormac were getting on, seeing that William had been gracious enough to come and help them out. Except after this morning's encounter he felt disinclined to look for William right now. He knew for certain he should be preparing his Chapter address for the next day, especially if the bishop would be sitting there. He had more correspondence waiting his attention than he liked to think about, and suspected some of it might be urgent in view of the many guests imminently expected. He tried to think of one thing he could face doing, and rejected everything. His feet took him back to his lodge; once inside he shut out the world and the community. Except his esquire, who had been polishing the table, and looked up, a waxy rag in his hand.

John stood, indecisive, staring at nothing. Brother Tom waited.

"It's chaos, Tom," the abbot said in a low voice, "inside me. I don't know what's happening. I'm overwhelmed. I've lost the thread. Everything seems to be thrown into muddle and confusion. Making it up as I go along. I feel as though Christ gave me one sudden push that sent me flying down from the safety of the riverbank into the boiling white water of the abbacy. Somewhere above me I heard his voice, faint and remote, calling 'Good luck!' And ever since I've been flung about, over my head, barely a chance to get my head above the surface to take a breath, no living possibility of any footing, no guarantee of even coming through at all… just… a mess. Everyone's angry with me. I've lost my dignity. I've made a complete ass of myself. It's bigger than I am, what this obedience asks of me. No room to put a foot wrong, everyone watching – oh, God in heaven! I just don't want to do this any more."

Tom listened. He felt the acrid bitterness and desperation of a man who'd had too much, and hesitated to reply. Good counsel, in his experience, generally made everything worse and was ill received. But his abbot looked up at him and said, "Help me, Tom."

This was the curious privilege of the obedience of abbot's esquire. The role required him to be hidden, effaced, patient. But there were moments – he remembered the terrible intimacy of Peregrine's infirmary room; "Help me, Tom." This he'd heard before. It asked a steadiness of faith that he had to reach deep within to find; not the platitudes that served to maintain everyday cheerfulness, something deeper than that. Something honest. He felt John's eyes upon him, and he looked at the ground.

"It's come to me," Tom answered his abbot, "when I've felt near despair, that Christ is not somewhere else – if you see what I mean. I've reached out for him at times, outside myself to where I thought he must be, and found only emptiness. There have been occasions when my calling hung by a thread; just a frayed, worn, faded thread between one possibility and the next. Without meaning and without hope. And I've wondered then if the whole pilgrimage came to nothing more than an inflated sense of self-importance – aggrandizement, to think my life might have significance, even purpose. I talked to Francis about this once. He smiled, and he said, 'Gethsemane.' That was all. But he hugged me. And Father, I'm wondering – now, you know me, I'm no scholar; I didn't get this from any book, just from a place past giving up, so I could have got it all wrong. Maybe you'd do better to ask Theo; he reads. But what I'm wondering – this white water – well, I've half an idea that the rocks are Christ and the torrent is Christ; that the terror is his, and the devastation. I think – maybe – he's not on the bank, and he won't be throwing you a lifeline, either. Because this is actually *it* – him – the reality where we find his real presence. And if that's true, which I know it might not be, then perhaps the thing to do would be to stop looking for a way out, and find the way in. A kind of surrender. If that makes sense."

Abbots who needed to talk seemed to have plagued Tom's working days more than he thought was his fair share. He did urgently have to make time to get up onto the moor and finish cutting the bracken they would need to make the preparations for building the ricks. He'd thought, once he'd finished tidying up in here, with the bishop out of their hair for five minutes he'd have the rest of the morning free to go, if they were quick. He hadn't anticipated listening patiently to John's private woes.

He dismissed his impatience and reluctance as unconfessable sin simply needing to be buried, ashamed of himself. The obedience of abbot weighed as a terrible burden on any man, and was not something anyone in his right mind would think of consenting to, in Tom's opinion. Which he thought probably explained why both abbots God had entrusted into his care as their esquire had spent a disproportionate amount of their time not exactly in their right mind.

He wondered – feeling guilty to even consider it – if William would be willing to come and take this on.

Meanwhile his superior nodded in dejected affirmation. "Aye, for sure. Christ is in all of it. Thank you, Brother. If you've finished in here, would you mind doing something for me? Will you go and make sure William has all he needs in the checker, and that he's turned up nothing that needs my eye casting over it? I'm aware it's been hard to get my attention these last few days."

Depends who you are, thought Tom; but felt entirely certain any such quip would be sourly received. So all he said was, "That's exactly where I was thinking of going."

He opened the door to the abbey court, stepped out onto the threshold, then leaned in again to say, "Uh-oh! Bishop's back. Headed your way, I think, Father."

He thought he had never seen any man, anywhere, look so wholly dismayed. The abbot just stood still and shut his eyes.

✠　✠　✠

"I want to put some questions to you, young men." The bishop raised his forefinger and leaned towards them. Theodore had compromised his jealously protected teaching circle to the extent of opening it out into a horseshoe, allowing the bishop to stand at the front and loom over his charges. Alongside his Lordship stood the abbot, who had made himself available as promised, and the novice master. Brainard had gone to make a nuisance of himself elsewhere.

"The religious life," explained the bishop, "is an unending quest – not for sanctity alone, but for knowledge and understanding. Ever deeper we must search the texts at our disposal – whether they are the writings of great scholars of the church, the holy Scriptures themselves, or contemporary debate from schools of thought only now being established. You agree with me, Father Theodore?"

He turned to look at Theo, who murmured his assent.

"Your novice master thinks as I do!" The bishop drew back his lips in a distinctly unnerving smile. "Well, then let's see what you've learned. Can you tell me, young man," he asked, fixing Brother Benedict with his eye, "whose student was Alcuin of York?"

Benedict looked at him blankly. "I – I'm so sorry, your Lordship," he admitted, darting a nervous glance of apology in his novice master's direction, "I don't know. Oh – that is to say – I can't remember."

"Anyone?" The bishop let his gaze sweep round the circle.

"He studied under Archbishop Ecgbert," said Brother Felix.

"Ah!" The bishop turned his attention to the source of this knowledge. "A scholar, eh? Tell me then, did he live in York all his life?"

"No, my lord. He went to the court of Charlemagne, from where he became abbot of Tours," supplied Brother Felix.

"Indeed!" The bishop pulled a face of surprised approval. "Then – anyone – whose work is *The City of God*?"

Felix hung back. "Boethius?" extemporized Brother Boniface; but the bishop shook his head long and slow. "Not Boethius."

"St Augustine wrote *The City of God*," Felix eventually said. "Boethius wrote *The Consolation of Philosophy*. Among other things."

"Well!" The bishop turned to the abbot and novice master at his side. "At least somebody's been paying attention!" He turned back to the silent circle of anxious novices. "What's your name, lad? Brother Felix? Right, then, you keep quiet. Let's hear from the others. Who can tell me, where in the Scriptures is it written, '*tu es Petrus et super hanc petram aedificabo ecclesiam meam*'[2]? And what does it signify?"

They did better on this. Cassian acquitted himself creditably with some vaguely apposite remarks about the apostolic succession. The bishop listened keenly.

"Very well," he approved. "And, '*Solvite templum hoc et in tribus diebus excitabo illud*'[3]?"

Brother Benedict showed himself equal to this, and thankfully had understood it to be in reference to the resurrection. The bishop nodded. "And where is it written, '*in principio erat Verbum*'[4]? An easy one!"

"At the beginning of John's Gospel, my lord," offered Brother Boniface, keen to redeem himself. But again the bishop shook his

2 You are Peter, and on this rock I will build my church – Matthew 16:18
3 Destroy this temple and in three days I will raise it up – John 2:19
4 In the beginning was the Word... (from John 1:1)

head long and slow. "Come on, lad!" he said. Brother Boniface looked puzzled, as did Brother Felix.

"Do you not know?" The bishop looked round the group, his eyebrows raised in enquiry. "Oh, come, come! Those are the first words of the holy Scriptures – the opening words of the Bible, from the book of –?"

An uneasy pause followed this question. Finally Brother Cassian spoke up. "The book of Genesis is the first book in the Bible, my lord," he said, "but…"

His novice master shifted slightly, just the smallest motion of his hand, but he fixed Cassian with such a glare that the novice closed his mouth at once. If Bishop Eric had made a mistake, it was more than their vocation was worth to point it out. So they accepted the inaccuracy that the Bible opened with words penned by the Evangelist, with no demur.

There followed further examination of their familiarity with the Scripture, in the light of its relation to the teaching of Holy Church. The abbot thought they made a good showing. After that, the bishop only wanted to know if they persevered in private prayer and whether their food was adequate. At last he expressed satisfaction with what he found, complimented the novice master on his good work, and looked expectantly at the abbot, ready to move on. As he held the door open for his Lordship to pass through, John looked back, hoping to catch his novice master's eye; but Theo would have none of it. Evidently he still felt disgusted at his abbot. More unhappy than he could ever remember being, John followed Bishop Eric across to the scriptorium, his next port of call.

Not until after Terce did John find himself alone. Even in the relief of solitude, he could not settle. The damage to his back had subsided to an inescapable raw soreness. He could just about bear it if he didn't forget to hold himself straight. He thought he owed it to his Lord to spend some time in prayer and study of the

Scriptures, but couldn't concentrate or apply himself to reflection. He drifted, turning over documents on his table, thinking about the minstrels due to arrive any day, wondering how long the bishop planned to stay, looking back on his conversations with the Bonvallet family, asking himself if he had done everything imaginable in service of the impossible task of assisting Hannah's passage into their midst. He thought he might go for a walk, but knew if he set foot out of his house he'd be besieged within minutes by people needing his attention. He wandered across his atelier, and stood by the fireplace. He raised an arm without thinking, in long habit of leaning his forearm against the stone lintel, resting his head against his hand, looking down into the fire. But today it hurt too much, and there were only ashes. And then came a knock on the door to the abbey court. John almost didn't answer. He felt wretched, and spent. But then, with a sigh, he went to open the door. And there (at Tom's request) stood William.

"May I come in? Are we still friends – after this morning?"

"I most sincerely hope so," said John. "I'm relying on your lifetime's tolerance of appalling behaviour making you understanding of my own.'

As the familiar luminescence of wry humour gleamed in William's features, and he turned to latch the door firmly shut behind him, John suddenly felt such gratitude for his company. He could not imagine anything human nature had to offer could shock or surprise this man. Right now, he was the only soul John wanted to see. "Come and sit down," he said.

Seeing John take not a chair but a stool, on which he sat gingerly and very upright, William also passed by the chairs; but he seated himself on the stone flags of the hearth, leaning his back against the wall of the chimney breast. For a while, they shared the company of silence. William traced curves in the soft grey ashes with first this finger then that, leaving space for John to speak when he wanted to.

"William," said the abbot eventually. "Love... married love... I mean – the way of a man with a maid... do you think... are we complete without it? Is it too beautiful a thing to miss? Does renouncing do violence to what God intended? Were we *made* for love? Now you have been a married man, what do you think about it?"

John watched his friend narrowly. He couldn't bear the thought that this should occasion embarrassment or evasion. These long years he had lived in celibacy, he had dodged and run from the natural bodily passions of a man. He wanted to have a straightforward conversation about it without anyone feeling the need to mutter warnings of the concupiscence of women, of the sin of Eve, of women's predilection for dragging the noble souls of men into the dread fires of hell.

The quietness of William's face remained unruffled. His hand continued to describe slow circles in the ashes as he thought about John's question.

"The way of a man with a maid?" he said. "Are you sure you want to talk about this, John?"

"Why?"

"Well... because... look – I'm married and you're not, and I don't want to make things worse than they already are."

John stared at him. "What's that supposed to mean?"

William nodded, accepting the defensiveness in his friend's voice. "All right then," he said. "So, the congress between man and woman? Coitus? What do I think about carnal knowledge? Where to start? I suppose I think not all such encounters are the same. Every pairing, every occasion, has a unique quality. Madeleine and I... well... when I first met her she had been heartlessly violated by a whole mob of men. I'm not even going to add to that injury the insult of asking the question if there could have been – for her – anything in the occasion beyond terror and pain and disgust. I can't bear to think of what she

130

suffered, and I cannot imagine how she found the strength within to move on from there to where we are now.

"But I have asked myself the question: what was in it for those men who attacked her? Did they find enjoyment in that? And if they did, was it the pleasure proper to the knowledge of a woman – do they even have an inkling of what such sensitive, delicate felicity can be? I suspect, for them, it was more like whatever my parents got from knocking the living daylights out of me when I was a child. Something in the experience kept them coming back for more. I guess you could call that pleasure. And my novice master, who laid the scourge on me every chance he could create, every time I put a foot wrong and sometimes even when I didn't. He got something out of it, of that I am sure. And maybe the men who raped Madeleine never asked themselves if there might not be more to coupling than just ramming home what you have into whoever has to lie there and take it. Poverty, eh?"

He paused, and glanced at John who sat, his face lined and bleak, worn out by the muddle of his confused emotions, his pain and the strain of responsibility, but listening intently.

"But then, if you look at how things were with me and Madeleine during my time in the community here, that's a different level of experience; but it had also no pleasure in it. On the contrary, it was absolute bloody torture. That one night I stole for an illicit visit to her house – and was seen, wouldn't you know it? You can't move hand or foot or shed a tear or twitch an eyebrow here but somebody sees and takes note, as you now know for yourself all too well! But, that night, was it pleasure? Even when I took her in my arms, I could feel such a howling sorrow of grief inside me, that I couldn't have this, would never see it through – not coitus I mean, but *life*, relationship. Because, obviously, I didn't know at the time that Mother Cottingham would leave us the means to be together. Besides, I felt so bad, so guilty, about going behind your back, and living a double life, when this community – who'd had such

131

doubts about taking me in – had done me the honour of trusting me. So, that hour or so she and I had together, was that pleasure? Not really. Urgency, desire, longing, hunger – but mostly what it all added up to was sheer misery, for a very long time.

"But if you look at the first time she and I came together as man and wife, well that's a different story. Neither of us… we weren't accustomed – weren't practised – we hadn't… it was new. But what I remember is not clumsiness or fumbling, but astonishment at how totally it possessed me. There was not one cranny of my being left uninvolved. It penetrated – odd that, you think as a male you'll be the one doing the penetrating – into the very heart's core of the man I am. Body, soul, the whole of me. For all I've been trounced and terrified from the earliest days I can remember, I never felt more wide open and defenceless in all my life. Nothing held back, you know? Every fragment of who I am, engaged and poured out. It shook me. I hadn't expected it. But to find myself received, loved, embraced – *desired*, John! – all of me; I tell you, it was so healing. It opened up a channel of singing hope. It was bliss, because it had nothing covert, no duplicity. That was its peace, its happiness. That was at the core of its pleasure. The openness."

He stopped, looking carefully into his friend's face, sensitive to the unfulfillable yearning John was painfully living through.

"But then, you know it well," he went on gently, "just as entering a woman can happen without love, so also love can flourish without any kind of carnal knowledge. I have a memory – it was so excruciating I can hardly look at it – the day I had to come to Chapter and tell this community I'd invested their entire store, without permission, in a ship that had sunk. Oh, God, what it did to me! Afterwards, I sat there until I thought everyone had gone, and it was safe to slink away. Who should be waiting for me in the doorway but Brother Thomas? Words cannot express how that scared me. He's a big man. I thought there'd be nothing left of me

132

but a smear on the ground like a morsel of dropped liver trodden on by accident. When I saw him standing there, my head reeled; I almost threw up. He read the look on my face, and he said, 'Oh, you prize idiot! What did you think I was going to do to you?' And he wrapped me in his arms, and held me close, let me dissolve. Brother Thomas; rough, very male. That was surely not carnality, but it was the most intensely intimate encounter. It's right up there with some of my moments with Madeleine as the means by which healing has seeped into my soul. Same with times when Michael has tended to me in the infirmary, and you have broken all the rules to give me Eucharist, and to bless my marriage to Madeleine. These are the things that have touched the quick of my spirit, redeemed me. It's the love that makes them beautiful and good.

"Now look, in your case you have come to the place in the wood where the path divides. You have fallen in love with this woman – right?"

John turned his face aside, ashamed, and moved his hand in a gesture of defeat. He said nothing.

"All right. Well, everyone tells me I'm no theologian, so don't expect any great insights here, but isn't there a thing in the epistles of St Paul where he makes a distinction between what's just his opinion and what is, as he puts it, 'from the Lord'?"

"Yes," said John. "There is."

"I thought so. Then hear this, my brother-in-law, because in my best judgment this is 'from the Lord'."

John looked at him then, intrigued.

"Being in love is good. It's healthy. It's nothing to be ashamed of. To my considerable surprise – by which I mean, I was completely gob-smacked – I discovered that Jesus is in love with me, William de Bulmer; filth-clot, dirt-slime, useful for something to sneer at. He *loves* me. I know, because I felt it. His presence to me was dignity. His love let me hold my head up, without pretending. And, not unreasonably, I am also in love with him.

133

"Being in love with someone is a wonderful thing. To have seen their humanity and found it beautiful, adorable, darling, captivating, delectable. Seeing another human being as – apparently – Christ sees them all, the whole time. It's a glimpse of heaven. So, nothing to be ashamed of there. I think you should rejoice in it, not beat yourself silly. Leave your scourge under the bed and let it gather dust. Or if we're thinking of that barbaric instrument of torture Columba left behind, on the river bed where I flung it. And, for what it's worth, I have found – the best answers to our dilemmas don't really come in talking it through or in soul-searching. They turn up by themselves, if you give them space and silence. I think you know that.

"But, so look, if this is your fork in the path – what to *do* about it? Which way to take? I know I've no right whatsoever to preach to you about maintaining chastity. My personal integrity is an object of derision. But… John… the men of this community have done you a great honour in trusting you to be their abbot. And my understanding is that you have a true vocation in the monastic way; by which I mean, it's *who you are*. If you chuck it in, you will be turning aside from the path of your own soul, the thing you came here to do. Not only that, Madeleine wasn't actually married to someone else. Rose is. Sure, I broke my vows and I'm an utter disgrace and everyone tells me so and I am in no doubt about it. But – another man's wife, John? You *have* to let it go.

"The thing I want to propose to you is that it's possible to be in love with someone without possessing them. Not try to crush it and despise it as something sinful, because it isn't. Usually these encounters have some mutuality to them – I'd wager you make her heart beat a little faster, as she does yours. Can't you maybe just rein in a bit? I mean, the choice need not be between sending her packing and having an affair – surely? Can you not delight in her, be glad of your humanity, receive the compliment that she likes you, offer her the affirmation that she is lovely – and leave it at that? Is it not possible to exercise restraint but just pass up all the self-loathing and toxic shame?"

Hesitantly, slowly, John nodded in affirmation. "I... you mean..."

"I mean loving the moon in the sky but leaving it there. Because even suppose you managed to bring it down, that would make earth darker not brighter, however good an idea it might have seemed when you first entertained it."

Again, John nodded. "Thank you. Thank you, William. There is no one else I could have –"

A loud, impatient rapping at the door interrupted him.

"Oh, heaven! I know that knock. Bishop's equerry. Can you disappear into my chamber while I deal with him? In case the bishop follows hot on his heels."

William accepted the wisdom of discretion, but thought he had better things to do than while away the afternoon trapped for an indeterminate period of time in John's bedchamber; so instead, he slipped out of the small door by the scribe's desk. Outside he paused, listening for the voices within. Once satisfied that the bishop's was included among them, he took himself off to the guesthouse to offer his help with preparations there.

He didn't see John for the rest of the afternoon, and the bishop dined with the abbot that evening. Since his Lordship was back, William sat in a niche at the edge of the shadowed nave during Compline, from where he could hear John but see little of him. He felt concerned for his friend. As the men trod with peaceful decorum from the choir, William stayed in his sheltering nook. When he had the cavernous building to himself, he walked over to the statue of the Sacred Heart of Jesus standing, arms raised in blessing, by one of the pillars. He lifted a slender candle from the pile set out for those who came to pray, lit it from the light that burned all day beside the statue, and set it firmly in the stand.

"John's struggling," he whispered. "He's drowning. Of your great kindness, merciful Jesus, give him a breathing space. Before we all regret it. Please. There's too much on. In your mercy – look – can't you just get rid of the bishop?"

He could think of nothing more to say, and after a moment's respectful pause, began to walk away. Then he turned back, looking up at the statue's grave, serene face. "I didn't mean in any final sense. Although… Well, really I just meant, could you get him out of here? The bishop. Not John. Please. Please."

Conscious that a year away from the daily round of liturgy had not improved the fluency of his praying, William left the matter in the care of the Sacred Heart. He resolved to tuck himself into the cleft between the church wall and the chapter house in the morning – if they'd left the door open, that is – to evaluate John's state of mind from his Chapter address.

The next day dawned sparkling and unclouded. Keeping close to the solid, imposing wall of the church, noting that the small door had indeed been left ajar, William found his hiding place, from where he could hear remarkably clearly – the brethren shuffling in, the reading from Benedict's Rule, and then the abbot's voice, steady and firm, carrying conviction but, William thought, entirely devoid of joy.

"My brothers, there's something I want to say to you. Not very polished. Only what's been on my mind. Something about suffering.

"You might think a man like me has not suffered enough to deserve an opinion, and if so you'd possibly be right. My life so far has been, by comparison with many others, easy. I was never destitute, nor subject to the cruelty of human violence. Even so, I have occasionally descended into hopelessness.

"When the example of holy suffering is held before us – Christ on the cross, or the holy martyrs – the word 'noble' seems to apply. So, we give thanks for 'the noble army of martyrs'. Sawn in

136

two, torn to pieces by lions, stoned to death… giving thanks to God, and holding their heads high in courage. Noble.

"Well, I've never been anything like that, I'm not noble at all. The worst wild animal that's ripped into my viscera has been the profoundest sense of inadequacy you can imagine. To be a failure, as a monk, as a disciple, as a man. Sometimes I've thought. Painful. So very painful.

"In this, the hardest, most terrifying thing, left me in free-fall, has been a feeling of absolute pointlessness – that it was all for nothing. Not noble, but not even useful, not directed or channelled into any worthwhile endeavour. Only the result of being human, being alive. Pointless.

"When I reflect on this, a picture of Christ on the cross comes to mind – 'My God, my God, why have you forsaken me?' It seems even he encountered that terrible state of meaninglessness, where what you thought it was all for simply evaporates. And then, his words, 'I am thirsty.' The unadorned human condition, taken down below the embellishment of values, beneath the complication of mission, without the dignity of significance. Just thirsty.

"Obviously, there are no options beyond living through such times. If I look at myself and see no achievement worth mentioning, see only one great big immovable disappointment of a man, aspiration deflates.

"But my job here is not to share around a counsel of despair. That wouldn't be very helpful, would it? So gazing into it bleakly, I have to pull out of it something to place into your hands – your hearts – because you trusted me. You made me your abbot, and that means it's my job to come up with something. I hope I'm not speaking too frankly. As you can probably tell, I haven't prepared this."

Outside in the morning air, William listened carefully. Inside, in the gathering of Brothers, Tom raised his head and looked across the room at his abbot, concern in his face. This didn't sound too good. But John, his hands held loosely in his lap within the big sleeves of his habit, sitting quietly straight, did not meet anyone's gaze. His eyes seemed to see nothing.

"And I prayed, 'Help me, Jesus', as I so often do. It's never let me down, you see, that prayer; never once. 'Oh, help me, Jesus.'

"And what came to mind was two thoughts that have threaded through the last few weeks, for one reason and another. I'm sorry; I'm not putting this well, am I? Anyway: the first is that whatever's going on in my own life – whether my faith is soaring and I'm overflowing with inspiration, or whether I'm in despair; whether others look up to me or I am disregarded, of no account – whatever – I have the option to be kind. It's a small thing, you would think, would you not, to be kind? Well, it is in the sense that you don't have to be rich or important, or very bright, to be kind. Even a little child can be kind. Even a dog. But it's no small thing to be on the receiving end of kindness. And the withholding of simple kindness is a root of bitterness and the seed of war; it causes the most terrible suffering. To look without compassion on another's life; to be unkind. Making the choice to be kind prays 'Thy kingdom come', even when you feel past praying and past caring.

"Kindness, I have found, for all it is small and ordinary, has a way of leading me out of safe territory. There's nothing like kindness for compromising righteousness and getting my religion and propriety all in a muddled knot. Kindness makes hay of many plans. But it is, I have come to believe, the currency of Christ's kingdom, the stuff out of which new hope can be made. Where we push a sprig of it into the earth in whatever place we are, life springs anew.

"So when all light is gone and the horrible sense of pointlessness overwhelms me, showing me my own inadequacy, I can at least make the choice to be kind; and that's my prayer, my creed, my way of anchoring myself to Christ.

"And the other thing – it caught my attention when someone

said it to me a few days ago – is about offering the gift of happiness. That having the power to make someone happy might be seen almost as a charism. Like working miracles. Like healing.

"In one sense, of course, you cannot make anybody happy. Each of us is responsible for developing contentment and gratitude, appreciation, as a state of mind. Happiness – we all know this – is not a destination to be reached or a goal to be achieved; it's the choice you make, the path you tread, the attitude you embrace. And that's no small thing, either. Happy people make the world happy, are good to be around, lift others up. Cheerfulness; it's a kingdom thing: 'Rejoice in the Lord always.'

"But a friendly word, reaching out to include someone, knowing their taste in food and offering a nibble of something they enjoy – even leaving them in peace, sometimes; there are so many ways to offer ordinary everyday gifts of happiness.

"So I thought, between choosing kindness and offering happiness, I could find enough to be going on with, a ladder up out of inadequacy and despair. It didn't matter what I'd been or done, or who I was or who cared, who saw or who knew. I could still do it. The thing is, when I feel really low, vision and inspiration are beyond me. But, you know, even when almost everything seems too much to manage, perhaps I can at least try to be kind. And I thought, that could give some meaning, something worthwhile, even to the most impoverished life. Even to mine. Sort of life compost, kindness and the giving of happiness could be; something in which faith and meaning could potentially thrive. It is only a small thing – I understand that. But sometimes I have to hope it will be enough."

His friend sounded bleak and enduring, William thought, as he concluded with complete absence of élan: "There's no big scholarship there, no expositions or dissertations or any of that. It just seemed useful to me; and so I thought it might be to you as well. Anyway, let's keep silence a moment."

Chapter Five

"My lord bishop has a particular request for dinner, since all these folk are gathering and this will be his last night here – it is a dish he relishes and it gives much amusement among the guests. He thought it might prove some pleasant entertainment and lift everyone's spirits to a jocular mood – saintliness smiles, remember!"

"What does he want?" asked Cormac, his tone cautious and the smile LePrique was looking for entirely lacking.

"It's an outdoor repast," explained the equerry, "just right for a summer evening. It cannot be served indoors because of the ring of fire. Goose roast alive is the delicacy."

"You've lost me." Cormac gaped at him. "You can't... how can you...?"

"Oh!" Brainard chuckled. "The dish is new to you? I'm sure your Brother Conradus will be familiar with it – his grandfather was the king's pastry cook, you know! Brother Conradus will have all the little tricks and flourishes at his disposal. It's quite simple. You pluck a goose while it yet lives, then you butter and lard it well. A duck will do, but there's more meat on a goose. You set it within a ring of fires, supplied with a bowl of water with salt and spikenel in it. He should have plenty of space about him, or the smoke will asphyxiate him and he will roast too quick. Don't be too hasty to get the fire ablaze, nor yet dally in kindling it – he mustn't get away! As he starts to roast, he'll walk about – seeking an escape you see, this is the merriment. Finding no refuge from the heat, he will drink the water to cool his inward parts, and the dose in it will cause his guts to loosen and void. The cook must watch over all, damping the bird's head with a sponge from time to time. Eventually he will run mad as his body cooks and he finds no respite. You must look for the moment he stumbles, for this is a sign that his heart is failing – and haste is needed then to take him to the table before he dies, else he will not still live when you pull off his parts one by one, to eat him up before he is dead."

In utter silence the two men in the checker heard this description. William, so white his skin seemed almost green, swallowed convulsively and pressed the back of his trembling hand firmly against his mouth. Cormac's eyes swam with tears; then his horror crystallized into concentrated fury.

"*Smile!*" urged the equerry, looking from one to the other of them. "Trust me, it is the greatest delicacy – once you try it you'll thank me!"

William tore his gaze from the smiling man and looked to St Alcuin's new cellarer – then despite the waves of dizzy nausea threatening to engulf him, he lurched forward with alacrity, alarm writ large across his face, into the space between the two men.

"Oh, for mercy's sake – he's not worth – *nay! Cormac!* Brother Cormac! *No!* Don't hit him, man! Great Queen of Heaven, have you taken leave of your –"

His presence of mind served its purpose inasmuch as Brother Cormac's fist slammed into the side of William's nose and not its intended target. The combination of trying to move too quickly while he was overcome with nausea, the sudden blow, and cracking his head against the table as he fell, left William in a crumpled heap at Cormac's feet, momentarily completely unconscious.

The equerry stepped back, his mouth dropped open in astonishment. As Cormac's adamantine blue gaze fixed him, he stepped back again, into the wall this time, turned and fled into the sunshine, bumping against the doorpost in his flight, throwing one startled glance of apprehension back over his shoulder as he hastened away, no longer smiling.

"Roast alive? By my soul, I'll roast *him* alive if he darkens my door again," muttered Cormac, dropping down on one knee to see what could be done for the collateral beneficiary of his ire.

Why in the name of all holy am I lying on the floor? was William's first thought on opening his eyes. Gathering his wits with an effort, finding Brother Cormac squatting in penitent concern at his side, he relocated himself into present reality. Dizzy and sick, he struggled to a sitting position, halted for a moment by the room still whirling around him. He focused hard on quelling the insistent waves of nausea. In his experience vomiting improved few situations. It took him a full minute to get his bearings properly, but once he had, he began to struggle groggily to his feet, shaking his head free of lingering giddiness. He clutched the table, swaying, willing himself back into clarity.

Cormac rose to his feet as William did, anxious for his wellbeing. "I am *so* sorry," he said. "I never intended…"

Ignoring the throbbing pain now asserting itself, and the rapidly diminishing vision in his left eye as it began to swell shut, William raised his head with a final shake and looked at Brother Cormac. "It's all right," he said. "I've had worse. But I suspect I had better apprise your abbot of this. LePrique will have run to his master and all hell will break loose here any minute now. What you must do – and quickly; go right now – is find Francis and make him stop whatever he's doing, without exception, to come here. Run through with him all we have in hand and make quite certain he has grasped at least the basics. Be sure, now. My guess is that within the hour neither you nor I will be free to work

142

on it any more. Hop to it, Cormac. His Lordship will be here breathing fire once this comes to light."

He was right. The equerry, boiling over with outrage and indignation, intercepted his reverend mentor in the act of sitting down to a light snack required to fortify him across the distance stretching between his breakfast and the midday meal.

That prelate heard with astonished displeasure LePrique's excited narrative of barbarism and irrational, unwonted – entirely unpredictable – violence. His full lips parted in perplexity as he contemplated the recountal that St Alcuin's cellarer had lunged at his manservant in a rage, intending to knock him unconscious, just because that harmless and well-meaning peon had faithfully represented his Lordship's requested preference for a poultry supper. A dull purple flush suffused his jowls above the tucked-in linen napkin. His brows knitted in stupefaction. *What?*

"By the grace of God," burbled on the incensed equerry, "that man who keeps hanging about was on the scene – he stepped in and took the blow, or by my estimation I –"

"What man?" cut in the angry bishop.

"Why, that – you must have seen him, your Lordship, he crops up everywhere – that bearded fellow. Dresses like a merchant. Lanky. Pads about like a fox. Unnerving, somehow. Long, sallow face. Late middle age. White hair. And the most disquieting blue – no, green – no, grey – very penetrating – eyes."

As he enlarged on his description, a new dawn of insight began to clear in the bishop's expression. For a moment the incomprehensible brawling LePrique had just depicted was dislodged from his thoughts as the question began to form – "This man… His name, LePrique? What is his name?"

"I… ooh… er… I don't think I know, your Lordship. He hasn't been introduced. He's not one of the brothers. He's just… sort of… there. Here. Around. I don't know who he is."

The bishop ripped the napkin from his neck. "Really?" he said.

"Well, I think I do. The character you just delineated fits one man and one man only that I ever knew. That's William de Bulmer. The very devil! What's he doing here? Maggot! Where is he? In the checker, you say? Well? What are you waiting for?"

Brother Dominic, bringing honey cakes and a dish of hot milk as instructed, was not a little nonplussed to find himself bearing them in just as his Lordship was impatiently hustling his equerry out of the guesthouse door.

The bishop surged across the abbey court to the checker, Brainard trotting alongside. They steamed in with all haste, but to their chagrin found only Father What's-his-name – the prior – at the cellarer's post.

"What's the meaning of this?" The bishop did not beat about the bush. "Where's your cellarer? Unless – LePrique – was this the man who tried to hit you?"

Francis's eyebrows rose in astonishment. He'd had but the sketchiest outline from Cormac, but had the wit to discern an emergency when it was presented to him, and got himself to the checker with all haste. "My lord?" he said, convincingly taken aback.

"Not you?" With a gesture of exasperation the bishop dismissed this particular line of enquiry – for now. It was, in any case, merely a sideshow, until he had caught up with his principal target.

"Are you harbouring here William de Bulmer?" His eyes, narrowed into gimlet points of light, bored into Father Francis with an inquisitorial intensity that would evidently have no truck with any equivocation.

"H-h-here?" Francis scanned the modest room in apparent mystification.

"In. This. Monastery." Through gritted teeth.

"But… Well, yes, we did…" Francis played for time. "We – I thought you knew, my lord. He was with us a whole year. He… It was after the great fire at St Dunstan's. He begged admittance – we took him in – but he –"

144

"Don't you play the fool with me!" The bishop glared, irate, at St Alcuin's prior. "Of course I know he was here. Of course I know he left. I know all about him. It's high time the consequences of his actions caught up with that man. He was a crooked, poisonous good-for-nothing since the roots of forever. But I gather he's contracted a marriage and attempted a suicide since last I clapped eyes on him. Before he's hanged for the felony of the second he wants excommunicating on account of the first. And, by God, if you're hiding him here I shall track him down because I mean to do business with him. Well? *Is* he here?"

At these words, something in Father Francis appeared to withdraw. Where a moment before he had seemed flustered, calm came over him now. He looked steadily at his interlocutor.

"Father William left us in the winter," he responded quietly. "Where he went, I cannot say. His whereabouts at the present time, I do not know. I cannot imagine who could have spread such a rumour of suicide. I am so sorry, your Lordship. I'm afraid I cannot help you."

For a long, roiling moment the bishop fixed Francis with his furious, silent glare.

"No?" he said then. "Well no doubt you will be happy for me to take a poke around for myself. Snap to it, LePrique. Let's run this fox to earth."

Out in the abbey court, his equerry close at his heels, the bishop paused and looked slowly about him in the sunshine.

"Well, well, well..." He spoke with soft satisfaction as his gaze fell upon the white hair of a thin man dressed in merchant's garb, but walking with the distinctive quiet tread of a monk, along the front of the west range that faced onto the greensward, towards the abbot's door. With the instinct of the watched, the man turned his head and glanced back over his shoulder. Realizing himself to be under keenest surveillance, he changed course, retracing a pace or two, ducking in through the door that led into the frater.

"*Taille haut!*" murmured the bishop; and set off in pursuit with a celerity LePrique would have estimated entirely beyond him.

The two men hurried across the court and into the refectory, deserted at the present time. They wove through the gaps between tables to cross the room and take the door into the cloister. There they paused, looking to right and left; which was when the equerry, glancing up the day stairs, caught a glimpse of their quarry disappearing.

William swore in silent fluency as he heard the first footfall on the wooden staircase. Fleet as a deer he slipped by the novitiate and the scriptorium, into the dorter. Now where? He noted without pausing, a second heavy set of feet added to the treading and squeak of the stairs. He passed the first three doors in the long corridor. Then, judging his time had run out, he made himself go slowly enough to lift the latch of the fourth door in silence. Slipping round the door into the cell, closing it noiselessly behind him, he turned to behold Father Chad, kneeling at his prie-dieu, gaping up at him in utter astonishment.

"Wh – ? What have you done to your eye?"

William raised his finger to his lips in warning, entreaty in his eyes, and Father Chad rose to his feet in bewildered silence, the question dying before he uttered it.

"I beg you, for God's sake, hide me," said William in swift undertone.

Father Chad closed his dropped jaw to frame the word "Where?"

But William, reaching down to whip the scourge out from under the low wooden bed – and Father Chad took a hasty step back – got down onto the floor and began to ease himself with all speed into the impossibly narrow space beneath the bed. Father Chad boggled.

"One of the many benefits of being skeletally thin," murmured William as he disappeared from view, pulling the scourge back under the bed after him. His face, grim and pale but for the livid purple of his bruised eye, glaring with its feral stare at Father Chad, was the last thing the monk beheld as, "Chad! Back to your prayers!" the spectre breathed in desperate urgency before disappearing entirely from view as the latch rattled and the door opened again – this time with considerable éclat.

"Where is he?" demanded the equerry, the bishop puffing in his wake, his face red-swollen with rage.

"Wh-who, my lord?" quavered the mild-faced monk, rising once more from his knees to face the invasion. "Me?"

He wondered whether he was supposed to be smiling, but somehow this didn't seem to be the moment.

"Where have you hidden him?"

Father Chad was a simple, honest man, not given to subterfuge or guile. His genuine stupefaction at unfolding events still registered in his shocked face as he gave the best performance he could muster.

"Where could I... who?..." He stared at them as the equerry pressed his point. "Under the bed? Is he under the bed?"

The bishop dismissed the suggestion with a snort of derision, but he did nonetheless stoop down to see. The floor was a long way down and kneeling uncomfortable for a man of some *avoir du poids*, so he made do with leaning one hand on the scratchy blanket covering the hard mattress, groping with the other into the dark space below the bed. He pulled out the scourge as it offered itself to him, and flung it to one side, pushing upright. In the baffled, angry silence that followed, no sound was heard but the two men breathing hard. A bishop does not like to be made to look foolish.

"It seems you were wrong." His chill tone added to the equerry's frustration.

"He went along here! He *did*," he insisted. "I saw him as I came to the top of the stair!" He pushed past Father Chad to the

147

narrow casement window, latched open on this warm summer afternoon. "Did he get out this way? Did he?"

"Oh, don't be ridiculous!" expostulated his Lordship, getting irritable now. "You've made a mistake, Brainard. Just face it. We're wasting time. He's probably halfway to the stables by now."

Father Chad, looking from one to the other, his hands clasped at chest level, his face wan with anxiety and all thoughts of smiling forgotten, ventured: "If – if you could tell me who you were looking for, I might be able to help."

The bishop looked with calculating penetration at this timid monk. Was he capable of deception? Probably not. "William de Bulmer," he said heavily. "Is he here? In this abbey, I mean. Obviously not in this cell."

"He…" Chad's features puckered into a small, worried frown. Lying was wrong. How could he do this? "William de Bulmer was certainly a member of our community, my lords. But he left us."

Father Chad visibly quailed as Bishop Eric fixed upon him full attention.

"We have reason to believe," the bishop said slowly and deliberately, "that he is back. The rumour has reached me that he is married – to a woman." His equerry nodded in agreement at this, also fixing his eyes on Father Chad. And he wasn't smiling either. "I have also heard a whisper that during his time here, he tried to take his own life. Such a man should be first excommunicated, then publicly flogged, then hanged. He is an execrable, repulsive transgressor, saturated with sin, and it is high time somebody caught up with him and brought his reprehensible career to an end. Don't you think?"

Coldly observant, Bishop Eric watched for the monk's reaction. Father Chad licked his lips. Why? Why did people choose to be so cruel? Was not life already hard enough? Did not each day have trouble enough of its own, without the introduction of a manhunt? Bishop Eric and his equerry both held him in their stare of accusation. They had to find some vindication for the invasion of this cell, a compensation mitigating the humiliating withdrawal of simple failure.

Father Chad saw that some kind of response was awaited, and one that would meet the expectation of their outrage.

"Father W-William…" he stuttered. "Well – th-that is to say – if you tell me he's married, I suppose he's not Father William any more. William, then. But he – are you sure he is married? He… Well, who would marry Father William? He was not a very personable… I mean… I think ladies would not… He could be a little bit gruff. But –" The bishop was beginning to turn away in impatience. Clearly this pusillanimous monastic had no light to shed. Still, he waited to hear where Father Chad's "But" might lead.

"But this I can tell you," Father Chad persevered, lowering his gaze before the intimidation of theirs, his clasped hands sweating: "whoever told you Father William was a malefactor, had him wrong. I don't know if he got married after he left here. When somebody leaves, we no longer discuss them. They are dead to us. It is true he had an accident up on the farm during his time with us, but he was loved in this monastery. He was a trustworthy man, a good man. Humble. God-fearing. Why ever should such a one have wanted to hang himself? It must have been a mistake, an accident, that's all. He didn't want to die. No one ever clung to life with such tenacity."

The eyes he slowly raised to ascertain the effect of his speech on the silent men were full of dread. He did what he could to stiffen his shaking legs. He felt dizzy.

"Brainard," said the bishop, "let's go. You hear me, Father Whoever-you-are – Cedd, is it? Oh, Chad. Well, you hear me. If that miscreant shows his face in this abbey, I will find him. And when I do, he will answer for all his filthy sin and faithless wickedness – not to me and to the ecclesiastical court only, but to Christ his judge. That man's days are numbered. I won't be made a fool of, not by him or any man – and certainly not by you."

"Oh, my lord!" Chad's consternation was genuine. But the bishop offered him no reassurance. With a scathing glare and a curl of the lip, the equerry fixed Chad one last time before following his superior out of the room. It seemed that the smiling days had finished. Father Chad stood motionless, his head cocked, listening to their corpulent tread descending the stair. Then he let his breath out in a sigh, crossed the room and closed his cell door again.

He bent down and picked up his scourge, stood holding it loosely in his hands as he watched William's sinuous and cautious emergence from under the bed. Wearily, the execrable, repulsive transgressor pushed himself up to kneeling, to standing, and (with the eye still available to him) met Father Chad's gaze.

"Trustworthy?" he said, after a moment. "Good?"

The monk moved his head, his hand, in a slight indication of diffidence. "I know, I know. I believed it at the time."

William, catching the twinkle in his eye, appreciated for the first time that Father Chad had a sense of humour.

"Cobwebs and dust on your clothes," murmured the monk, reaching out to brush them away. Then he looked William square in the face. "I expect it'll be safe for you to go now," he said, "but I ought to own up: you've been on my conscience, ever since you left. It didn't take long before it dawned on me, we – well, I – missed an opportunity. I hope this changes things. I hope we may be friends from now on."

Under William's small grin, Chad saw the etching still of tiredness and fear. "I'll add you to my mental list of Men in this Monastery who have Saved my Life," William answered him. "And of course, yes – I am honoured to be considered your friend."

He turned to go then, but paused as he reached the door. "Look – you may not understand – I want you to know – all I ever, ever wanted was a peaceful life... security... shelter from the storm... for things to be comfortable, and... safe. But... well, it was such a struggle to get to that. I had to fight for it, tooth and nail. But I'm sorry – truly, I'm sorry, Father Chad – if you were one of the many who got bitten and scratched along the way."

Father Chad nodded, then drew breath with a certain resolve. William looked at him in enquiry. Father Chad hesitated, unsure in this mood of new bonding whether he should say what he wanted to, or just let it go. But William was waiting.

"I am glad we have put the past behind us," said the monk, averting his gaze, embarrassed at what he planned to say. "But..."

A certain tension entered William's entire demeanour as he braced himself for whatever this might be.

Father Chad ploughed bravely on. "Even so I must admit, Father William – at least... er... well – William – that it might be a wise course to take – for all of us, for you as well as us in the community – if after this you maybe don't come here any more. I know you mean your interventions kindly, but... before you came... Before... Until... Oh dear... A bishop's Visitation used to be a simple, uneventful, encouraging experience." He waved his hand desperately, feeling William's gaze upon him, watching, not moving. "Surely you must see –" there was no accusation in his pleading tone – "trouble always follows you."

He did not – could not – look at William, which was just as well because, if he had, he would have taken the wooden impassivity his words brought to the other's face as stubborn sullenness, hostility. For one moment they both stood unmoving; then, "I understand," said William softly. "I hear you." He latched the cell door quietly behind him as he left.

Edged as close to the stone wall as he could get beneath Father Chad's low wooden bed, flat on his back, unable in the

151

shallow space even to turn his throbbing head sideways, refusing the rising panic of claustrophobia, William had waited. It had occurred to him in the close prison of his meagre refuge that human history was peppered with terrified men cramped in choking hiding places desperate to escape discovery by their fellow human beings. He would not even look at the visceral wound left by Chad's plea that he leave and never return. It felt too painful, and he thought he'd better deal with it later, in some safe and private place. Wondering what it would be like to live in a world where people simply accepted and understood, he trod cautiously along the passage out from the dorter, every nerve strained for warning signs of human presence. But he was alone. As he went warily down the stairs to the cloister, he noted that his legs and belly felt weak, shaky. "Pull yourself together," he instructed himself silently, and gave thanks for an empty cloister as – keeping to the shadowed side by the wall, away from the light from the garth – he walked along it to the abbot's door. There he listened one moment lest there be voices within, before knocking.

✠　✠　✠

"You've got a visitor."

Abbot John swung round, but saw no one awaiting his attention. "Where?"

"In your chamber," Brother Tom explained. "I think he's in trouble again. He wouldn't say."

With a quick frown of puzzlement, the abbot crossed the room and went through into his chamber.

"Oh, God save us," he said, taking in the black eye, the tired, strained face, the dusty clothes, as William, sitting on the floor in the far corner of the room with his back to the wall, regarded him in silence. "What now?"

William shrugged, stayed where he was. As the abbot entered the room, the reflexes of William's muscles had bidden him stand; but he no longer belonged to this community or owed his brother-in-law the respect of his fealty.

"I don't know how word has reached his Lordship of my personal history," he said, his voice flat and despondent, "but he wants me excommunicated, thrashed and strung up – and perhaps for entertainment they'd like to tear off my fingernails or slit me open and wind out my entrails on a bobbin. Who knows? It is the felony of my attempted suicide that has so upset him – and how did he hear of that? Besides my desertion of my monastic vows, of course."

John listened to this in silence and stillness. William nodded in affirmation of the horror on his face. "I think you might shut the door," he continued, "because that's not all."

John turned back to the door and put his head round it. "Tom, I am not here," he said.

"Even to the bishop?"

"No – *especially* to the bishop. I am not here."

He withdrew into his bedchamber, and sat on the floor beside his friend, still moving carefully, and avoiding resting his back against the wall. "What else, then? Who hit you?"

William turned his wry grin towards the abbot. "I got between Brother Cormac's knuckles and their intended destination," he said. "I thought it best the bishop's equerry not be laid out cold in the checker. It had better be me."

John's mouth dropped ajar, and William began to laugh.

"Oh, my life!" the abbot exclaimed. "William, this isn't funny! For heaven's sake, what are we going to do?"

"About Cormac? Yes? Well, my counsel is that you make a big show of locking him up in your prison, full of expostulation and lurid declarations of how you'll flay him to ribbons just as soon as your busy schedule gives you space to put your mind to it. Tell 'em it'll do him good to go hungry in the cold and damp dark, contemplating the blood and pain and violence of the drubbing you mean to put him through. Surely the bishop can't stay here forever – there must be other monastery larders for him to empty somewhere in the ridings of Yorkshire."

"But… if Cormac's out of action, who's going to oversee all the provisions and paraphernalia of this confounded wedding?"

"I am, you numpty. I'll just stay out of sight."

John gazed ahead at nothing, chewing his lip, weighing this in silence.

"You… William, how could I ask it of you? I'd never forgive myself if they found you."

"Find *me*? I hope I've not lost my touch that badly. I've been dodging someone's wrath and malevolence the whole of my life. It's all I'm good for."

John sat quietly and thought, recalling to his mind the weariness in William's taut face but five minutes before. *Resilient*, he thought; *and brave.*

"You sound very confident," he said eventually, "that they will not find you."

"I am – and you know why? I have seen a confession of guilt and sin signed by a man after he was tortured. I knew his signature from before they got to him, too. The change in it was not something I would easily forget. Oh, no. They will never find me. Look, you've not too many choices, John. You can't leave Cormac on the loose after this, and the only other option is to go ahead and beat him to a pulp in Chapter – with a lash like that insult to the Creator you used on your own back – while his Lordship salivates and crows over the scene. Look, just put someone discreet and steady in the checker, and I'll nip in before first light and after dark each day to keep things on track."

"First light? It's May. When? Three in the morning? Is that

realistic? The sun doesn't go down until after nine o'clock, either. You will be sleeping when?"

"Oh, for mercy's sake, leave the details to me! Just be glad of the offer, why don't you? Concentrate on keeping your guests happy, and his Lordship occupied and separated from your cellarer by a nice stout door. Francis is sharp – he can man the checker for you until the bishop pushes off."

✠   ✠   ✠

John, knowing he could depend upon his brother-in-law for shrewd pragmatism, took his advice. When his cellarer cautiously presented himself within the half-hour, the abbot escorted him to one of the prison cells in the eastern range, each man apologizing to the other all the way. John turned the key himself, having encouraged Cormac to see it as locking the bishop out more than locking Cormac in. Abbot John felt definitely relieved to have secured that situation, but still conscious that this was the least of his problems. He might hope by determination and intelligence to remain elusive until suppertime, but sooner or later he'd have to face this reckoning. Whichever way he looked at it, he could not imagine what he could possibly say to get himself out of it, much less to keep William reliably safe.

He slipped back into the cloister, leaving aside for now the steadily increasing list of urgent tasks requiring his attention, and sought out the most shadowed and obscure nook the side chapels within the abbey churches afforded, there to pray most desperately for his Lord's immediate help. After some while of frantic prayer and racking his brain, John got up from his knees and went to find Brother Conradus in the abbey kitchens. He nodded pleasantly at Rose, but did not stop to speak to her. He went directly to his kitchener. "The bishop's supper," he pleaded. "Make us something magnificent, something delectable. Do your very best, Brother, I beg you. I cannot go into explanations, but I have to serve something that will mellow this man. We're in a hole, and I need every means at our disposal to climb up out of it. Something delicious, Brother Conradus, if you can. That thing you told me about, that Francis of Assisi asked for – er…"

"Ah! You mean Lady Giacoma Frangipane de Settesoli's delicious sweet," said Brother Conradus, nodding in understanding. "Fra Jacopa. The recipe my mother had. Yes, there's time to make that for his Lordship's supper if I don't delay. Don't worry, Father. I'll come up with something good."

And from there the abbot went back into the cloister and up the day stairs to the novitiate, where he begged a brief private audience with Father Theodore.

"Are you still angry with me?" he asked first of all.

Theodore shook his head. "No. You were doing the best you could, I know. It happens. I've got over myself."

"Good. Because I'm in another mess now, and I need your advice most urgently."

John related the events of the afternoon, explaining that so far he had been able to avoid Bishop Eric, but could only hope to keep out of his way until suppertime at the very latest. By then he would have to answer some very difficult questions about William – not only his present whereabouts but his time at St Alcuin's.

"What am I to tell him, Theo? He's going to be digging up all manner of inconvenient goings-on. He'll want to know what the devil I was playing at, letting William go. And what if he finds him? What if he finds Madeleine? What if he turns up the allegations of witchcraft – besides which they would both be adulterers in a church court, and I shudder to think… I don't know if… I mean, there's a trail of legal documents. I witnessed their marriage. Yes, I know it was stupid, but I did it. And Mother Cottingham left them their cottage."

Theodore listened carefully.

"Well," he said cautiously, when John stopped, the abbot's strained gaze beseeching wisdom and help, "witnessing their marriage may not have been the canniest choice you ever made. But only they have the document, yes? You didn't go into the church – just the lych-gate? No? Then I don't doubt that record is in the safest hands possible. And you could ask William to destroy it if you think it prudent.

"As for the cottage, as I understand it, Mother Ellen left it to Madeleine outright. The money, she bequeathed to Madeleine with a share to her husband should she marry. No man was named in that legacy. William's name came up only in respect of the money she left to us here at St Alcuin's. I very much doubt they'll have changed the title of the deeds – partly because William would be the last person to want to advertise his whereabouts, and partly because such a legal change couldn't be got without a hefty fee and – well, you know William. He'd do without. So, though rumours there may be, I think we may rest in good hope there's no legal trail to track him to earth."

As he spoke, the expression on John's face changed. First puzzled, then intrigued; then he said, "You seem to be more familiar than I had expected with the detail of all this! Was I the only man in this monastery not to know anything of William and Madeleine's affairs?"

Theodore smiled. "You were, without doubt, the last man they could trust with a confidence. But these things were not general knowledge. I was Madeleine's confessor. She left some secrets in my ear. Which will remain *sub rosa*. I'm only reminding you of what I think you already know. And, does it help?"

"Yes." John shook himself free of the suspicions and uncertainties the conversation had unexpectedly aroused. "Is that all? Have you got any other bright ideas?"

"Well… Only one, I think. The bishop is regarding William as a fugitive? An apostate? Yes? He assumes he left us by his own choice? All right, then. I wonder, does he know about the money? I mean about William taking it upon himself to invest our entire wealth in that ship that went down off Lizard Point. Because, look; I know you might not want to blacken William's name even further, but what about this? Toward the end of the sixth century, the Council of Auxerre decreed that if a monk stole money or had private possessions, his punishment should be expulsion from his own community to enclosure in another. As things were, could it be safe to assume that if William hadn't left here of his own volition at all, but you had thrown him out, it could arguably have been very hard to find another house that would take him in?"

Abbot John digested this thought, and the beginnings of a smile kindled in his eyes. He nodded in slow agreement. "Yes. I think that's very likely."

"Besides, we've had a papal exemption here for some fifty years – that's why we were able to elect our own abbot and confer your benediction ourselves. So I think the right of excommunication rests with you, not the bishop, because William's solemn vows make him subject to your authority, if anyone's, in this house. And his own place burned down, so he couldn't have stayed there even if he'd wanted to. The bishop's Visitation is a spiritual discipline we agree to – Father Peregrine thought it safeguarded against pride and obstinate ideas. An outsider's eye can see what the family misses. And he can complain about us of course – it certainly pays to keep him sweet. But I think you'll find you're answerable only to the Pope. I'm not sure I should have told you that, mind you; you might become insufferable from now on!"

John grinned at the joke, but absently, as he absorbed the information, heartily glad that his novice master had a good grip of church law and its nuances. He stood, taking it in, wondering with some embarrassment how this crucial facet of their governance, which he must have – well, at least *should* have – known, had passed him by. "Thanks, Theo," he said. "Thank you very much. Very well, then. Let's get to it. I'll do my best. Pray for me."

✠   ✠   ✠

Finding no trace of either the turbulent cellarer or the evanescent ex-monk, it was in very ill humour that Bishop Eric heaved into the abbot's house in search of supper that evening, Brainard LePrique following hot on his heels, still forgetting to smile.

Out of all the men in his acquaintance, John dearly wished he could have had William at his side that evening. His abbey was known and loved for its simplicity and humility, not its prestige. He had no one of significantly noble birth among his monks, nobody schooled to elegance of manner and finesse in conversation. The only men of them all who came of any kind of aristocratic family – and even then they were farmers – were his precentor Father Gilbert and Father Francis his prior. It was at least a comfort to have Francis there, chatting genially, quick to notice everything, attentive and courteous in every detail. Observing him in action, John saw how shrewd William had been in advising him to give Francis the obedience of prior. His presence brought a balm to any situation, and John felt the atmosphere lighten as Brother Tom and Brother Conradus brought in plate after plate of aromatically delicious delicacies cooked to perfection.

Brother Conradus had raided the wines provided for the wedding to delight the bishop's palate; he had, as promised, done his best – and it was good.

When, inevitably, Bishop Eric raised the matter of William de Bulmer, John tried to imagine himself into the mind of the man they discussed – how would he have handled this? How would he have weaselled out of it and left the bishop wondering what had

159

happened? Half-truths and political manoeuvring had never been John's style. But he gave it his best shot.

"My lord bishop," he murmured, as he thought maybe William might have done, "we are so grateful this has come up during the time of your Visitation. It was for just such occurrences that our foundation offered voluntarily to invite the spiritual friendship of such a wise mentor as yourself. We are exempted from diocesan authority, as of course you know – but nonetheless we value your guidance and counsel. I of all men feel the burden of responsibility. Mine is to decide when to censure and when to forgive. Mine is to decide – though I tremble at the solemnity of it – when to excommunicate if it comes to that. And how I value the comfort of your spiritual direction in coming to a mind. It all feels so new still. My lord, I thank you from my heart for all your help.

"But –" John lowered his eyes to avoid any impression of pugnacity or insolent confrontation, reaching for his wine and taking a sip before continuing. "But in the particular case of William de Bulmer, I think you may have been... not misled exactly, because your keen wit would soon see through any errors of judgment... Shall we say those who brought you word may not have known the whole story? Could that be thought fair?

"The thing is, before he came to us, William de Bulmer begged refuge at many doors. He was not a popular man. But in his time with us, we saw deep repentance, we saw him become malleable to instruction. Then in his eagerness to please us, to repay our kindness, as he saw it, he overreached himself. Set to assisting our cellarer Brother Ambrose, who was old and less quick-witted than in his prime, William de Bulmer saw – and seized – a risky opportunity to improve our wealth. He ventured to invest a large sum of money without my permission. Unfortunately the vessel bearing goods, for which he had taken it upon himself to pay out a goodly sum from our coffers, was wrecked, and all aboard lost. My lord bishop, you will instantly see the quandary this put me in. No religious house would take him, yet my duty was to expel him from our community – he had, in effect, stolen from us. He had appropriated the community's wealth and used it as private property. He meant us no harm, he meant it for our good – but it was a grave sin. The proper course of action was not excommunication, for he was not apostate and he did not seek to leave us. But the fitting punishment must surely have been expulsion from our midst. In the absence of any community that would have him, enclosure in another became functionally impossible. We sent him forth to fare as he might, like a scapegoat. God knows what became of him. If it is true indeed that he made a home for himself as an ordinary householder and took a wife, well, who could blame him?"

Bishop Eric watched John narrowly, weighing these words. Francis sat swirling his wine slowly in its pewter goblet, not looking up, his face thoughtful and composed, breathing peacefully, apparently relaxed. Brother Tom, tasked with waiting on their table, stood quiet and alert against the wall. LePrique watched the bishop watching the abbot. John waited, trying to look open and without guile. He wished he'd never left the infirmary. He wished with all his heart he'd let some other man take on this confounded job.

"I heard," said the bishop then, "de Bulmer tried to take his life."

John reared backwards, his face a picture of astonishment. "You heard what?" he said. "From whom? Tried to...? When? While he was with us? But – we were his shelter from the storm! Why would he have done that? From whom did you hear such a thing, my lord, may I ask?"

Francis and Tom remained entirely still. John hoped they saw, he hadn't exactly told a lie as such. He wondered if they would ever trust anything he said to them after this.

161

The bishop frowned. This thing was slipping away from him. "Is he here?" he asked abruptly. The abbot did a double take.

"Is he – de Bulmer? How do you mean, 'here', my lord? In this monastery? You have seen him? Recently you mean?"

LePrique thought he'd help. "There's a man my lord bishop says fits his description. Not a monk, a merchant – or someone who dresses as one. Thin and pale. Bearded. White hair. Unnerving gaze. Crops up everywhere. Foxy, watchful type."

Father Francis laughed, and the cheerful, pleasant sound of it eased the mood. "Oh, *him*," he said. "God bless us, my lord, I know the man you mean! And he *is* called William, too – well, isn't everybody who isn't called Thomas or Edward or John? I see how the confusion arose. Yes – he helps out with the provisions. I don't think he lives in the village, though – York man, I believe. He brought in some bits and pieces because we've a big wedding in the offing. I suppose you might have seen him in the checker? He'll have had some business to do with Brother Cormac, I imagine. William... William... oh... Fletcher, is it? Or Fuller? Brother Cormac would know. Yes, I came across him myself yesterday, and again this morning – I do see the resemblance. This was the man Brother Cormac regrettably punched, Father John. Had a black eye, poor soul. I had to apologize. I believe he's gone home now."

Brother Tom moved quietly forward, replenishing the bishop's wine, adding to his plate another serving of the chicken and salmon pastry, with its saffron rice and crisp, tender salad greens.

"But there was another matter," continued Father Francis easily, "that with my lord abbot's permission I wished to raise with you – if we've dealt with that? Yes? Moving on from Father William, then – whatever became of him, God bless him – I wondered if I might ask your advice, my lord bishop, about our school here at St Alcuin's. You've met our boys, and liked what you saw, I believe. As you know, we take not only the sons of

162

freemen, but the more promising from among the families of the poor. We teach them arithmetic and grammar, logic and rhetoric, astronomy, Latin, some French for those families in more elevated social circles, and music of course. Now, it's the music that has been exercising us. We have always taught them plainchant and simple melody. But, from France, we are hearing more and more of polyphony. Our dilemma is this: should we avail ourselves of the newest scores to be had, so we may pride ourselves that the education we can offer is the very best? Or should we, for the sake of spiritual lowliness and a humble heart, keep to the old ways and teach them the plainchant alone? Especially since some of them are hardly sophisticated."

Listening to this with some amazement, John hoped fervently there was at least a grain of truth in it. He could easily envisage the bishop taking his schoolmasters to task, and he hoped if they were as surprised as he was himself to hear of this, they'd at least have the gumption to disguise it. But he saw the keen interest that suddenly lit the bishop's eyes. Francis, evidently, knew his man. "Ah! *Ars nova* or *Ars antiqua*!" The bishop chuckled, transformed. "So you've entered the fray! What have you got? Johannes de Muris? Philippe de Vitry? Guillaume de Machaut? Well, now! His holiness Pope John had no time for it whatsoever, of course – not one bit! But times move on, seasons change. God rest his soul. And you say you're trying this on the boys in the *school*, as well as the choir? *Avant garde*, eh? Well, well, well!"

St Alcuin's prior did not seek his abbot's eye. He kept his gaze fixed steadily on the bishop, who was thawing nicely and grew increasingly expansive as he warmed to his theme. Brother Thomas refreshed his Lordship's wine. John could hardly believe this. They seemed to have got through.

Be that as it may, he thought William Fletcher or Fuller, or whatever name he now went by, had better keep close quarters in the hayloft until his Lordship lumbered off. And the same went for Cormac locked up in the abbey prison.

As their meal drew to a close, Brother Tom murmured in his ear: "Will I take some broken meats out to feed the foxes when I clear the dishes, Father?"

"Oh – surely."

And his esquire set to work quietly and unobtrusively lifting leftovers away, bearing the scraps of their supper out into the dusk while John had the bishop and his man still securely occupied over wine and conversation.

The abbot escorted his guests into the chapel for Compline as the bell began to toll, then turned back to speak to Brother Tom coming into the choir.

"All well?"

Tom hesitated. "With Cormac, yes. Grateful for his supper. Accepts the wisdom of his billet. But the other... that man has two familiar demons, Father: terror and despair. Tonight it's the latter has him by the throat, I'm not sure why. He didn't say much. He thanked me. But the misery seeping out of him – I don't know – he just looked very despondent. I suppose I would too, in his situation, but I got the feeling there was more to it than that."

John nodded. "It'll have to wait until the morning, I think; but then I'll go up there myself. Thank you, Brother."

He turned to go, but Tom put out a hand and caught his sleeve. He spoke low.

"I believe our prior has been busy. What Francis said to me this afternoon, I think he said to every brother in the house. Possibly even the novices, though he may have stopped at Theo and left him to deal with them."

"Which was what? I mean, what did he say?"

"Something along the lines of: 'The bishop – feed him, flatter him shamelessly, ask his advice, hang on his every word, gaze at him in admiration. And remember, if it comes to it, none of us – not one solitary man among us – has the dimmest, faintest, tiniest inkling of any idea whatsoever concerning the whereabouts of William de Bulmer. What became of him, if he married, where he lodged; we do not know. If a brother leaves this house, he is dead to us. We do not enquire, we do not pass any whisper. William de Bulmer was with us, he is gone – that's all we know.'"

John frowned as he took this in, and Tom added hastily: "Francis did also say to think about it carefully, to remember our vocation and try not to tell any lies."

"Oh, right," said his abbot, "that'll be easy, then! Very well. Thank you for letting me know. Come on; it's past time we began Compline."

✠   ✠   ✠

Not unreasonable on this May morning for the abbot of a monastery to pass by the stables, going about his business with a linen bag of provisions slung from his shoulder, located as they were so near the guesthouse. He paused, stopped to greet two or three horses watching him with interest over their half-height doors. He looked around in a casual manner, then he drifted aimlessly but without delay toward the ladder leading up to the hayloft above.

The warm, fragrant, dusty storage space boasted scant illumination. If the roof had been entire the twilight would have verged on darkness. Light entered only by the grace of slipped tiles here and there, the access hatch, and a small square window left in the stonework at the gable end. Scrambling into the loft, moving away from the ladder so he would not be visible from below, John more felt than saw himself observed. He stepped forward, allowing his eyes to adjust to the gloom from the contrast of the brightness outside. Eventually he made out his friend, sitting on the hay-strewn floor, his back propped against the stacked fodder.

"I brought you something to eat," said John, in an undertone.

"Thank you. Most welcome," came the hushed reply. John brought the bread and cheese and apples, the little stoppered leather flask of ale, which William received with a nod of thanks but no further words. Up here they had to be quiet; it was imperative William's presence remain undetected. Even so, John discerned something beyond that in his friend's stillness. Dejection, he thought. Something raw and taut and suffering he could perceive all the more clearly for the shadows and profound quietness. He squatted down before his friend, and his question barely broke the silence. "What? What's wrong?"

In the vague dusk he watched William shake his head in dismissal, gesturing briefly to avert the question. "Nothing. I'm fine."

John felt within himself the familiar sag of resignation. Clearly this was something that would have to be expertly teased out; patience required. Not too long, he hoped. The time he could spare for this was limited. He folded himself down to sit cross-legged, angled to make the most of such light as filtered upwards and gleamed down. Motes of dust drifted in the muted luminescence. John tried to see William's face. Evidently his friend intended to offer no help with that.

"Thank you," murmured William again, reaching forward to pick up the hunk of bread set before him. John leaned forward and wrapped his hand over William's.

"You *are* going to tell me," he persisted, still in an undertone, "because I need to know. Firstly because I'll have you on my mind all day if there's some fresh trouble but you don't tell me what it is. Secondly because it is badly on my conscience that you came here to help us and it's put your life at risk. Just spit it out, will you, because I shouldn't stay long but I won't go until I know."

William muttered a string of obscenities at him, encasing a suggestion that he might like to leave now, which John took as a hopeful sign of making headway. He took no offence at it; this was just William in a bad mood. He made no move to go. Gently, he withdrew his hand, and waited. He had his night vision now, enough to observe the bitterness etched on his friend's face as William leaned his head back against the hay behind him, one eye still swollen shut. "Come on," said John quietly. "It's only me. What is it?"

It was clear John meant to go nowhere until he had an answer.

"'Tis the merest thing. No more than…" William shook his head. "Don't concern yourself. It wouldn't even bother me normally. Yesterday was a difficult day – that's the only reason it got to me. And it was nothing, no more than that… someone – quite properly and rightly – suggested I make myself scarce. Go away. Not return. Leave and don't come back. Because I am trouble and bring trouble, and…" He stopped speaking, dismissed the thing in another irritable gesture of his hand. The day carried to them sounds of the monastery round about, the horses shifting, blowing, chomping on hay in the stalls below them, occasional voices in the distance, the tiny scratch and clatter of birds on the roof tiles above. But that was the world beyond the silence lying between them, enveloping them. The practised fingers of John's soul probed the mute pain.

"Who?"

"Oh… John… for pity's sake. Do you not think I am loathed enough without adding fuel to the fire?"

"Who? Look, I'll have this out of you, William. I will. If you do not tell me, I'll ask every man of them at Chapter. Who?"

"Oh, what? Between you and me, then, Father Chad. But he didn't mean it spitefully and he had good reason. I took refuge in his cell, under his bed, and brought the bishop and his lackey on him, breathing fire and damnation and leaving poor old Chad having to lie for me. Not his style. He was scared. He just wants me to go away."

"William? I'm sorry? You didn't tell me this. You say you were hiding from Bishop Eric under Father Chad's bed?"

"You got it."

John sighed. This mess seemed to be growing into something greater than he could see his way to encompassing. In such a pass he had learned, from many years in the infirmary, to ignore the encroaching litter of complexity and detail in favour of concentrating completely on human pain.

"Listen. For one thing, heaven only knows what kind of a pickle we'd be in right now if you hadn't come up here to steer us through. But more than that, you are my family – my brother-in-law. You and Madeleine are the only family I have. Nobody is going to order you away from here. William, I need you. I rely on you. I love you. In a world where almost no one can be trusted, I know I can trust you. When sorrow came to my life like some terrifying dark angel, you watched over me and saw me through. I'm the abbot of this monastery, and right and left all day long everyone wants something of me. In my whole life, you are pretty much the only man who asks nothing from me, and still is there for me. You've stood firm while I've shouted at you, turned my back on you, misjudged you. And you *never* judge me. Well – apart from you seemed seriously annoyed with me the other day, but set that aside. I don't know quite how this happened to us because we didn't have a promising beginning, but I can honestly say you are the truest friend I have in all the world. All right? My brother – my friend?"

And then William was glad of the shadows. Silently he lifted his hands to his face, leaning forward until he crouched there, hunched over, his knees drawn up to his chest, his head bent. Asked to guess, John would have judged it impossible that a man could sob so deeply without making the smallest sound. With practice, he supposed, you could do anything. In the hay-scented dusk the abbot sat and watched the faint blurring, betraying the tremors passing through William's body as his friend shrank into the familiar agony of his various levels of hell. The kindness had found him, touched and exposed the raw hurt, got past his efforts to splint it, dismiss it, not care.

When he could speak, "Thank you," he said, straightening up, lifting his head, wiping his nose on the back of his hand and rubbing his good eye with the heel of it. John did not offer the use of his handkerchief. He felt entirely sure William would prefer the fiction that he had never seen the tears.

William shook his head, ashamed that he could not keep his emotion contained.

"I'm sorry I've messed things up. And I'm sorry I swore at you," he said. "I'm sorry to make such a fuss over so slight a matter. I think I'm just tired. And... if I'm honest... I've been so scared. If they caught me – by the Mass, it doesn't bear thinking about. Even so, I should be able to bear myself more continently, be better in command of myself than this."

"Oh, I don't know," the abbot said, and William felt the comfort and kindness in his voice. "You'd be a terrifying man if you could be as invulnerable as you want to be. I'd say the capacity to feel is your saving grace."

"It is not," William responded, and John felt the force behind it, even though his friend still spoke carefully low. "My saving grace is the ability to come up with a strategy and work it through. My head is my strength and my heart is my weakness."

"William. You don't believe that. Come on. All you've learned here? Madeleine? Tom? Are the lessons of the heart held so lightly?"

"Well, then they have at least to be yoked together. My head and my heart: it's like the disciples of old quarrelling as they went along the road, arguing about which of them was the greatest.

My head says the shrewd thing is that he should be the master. My heart fights back. Seems it doesn't agree."

John smiled. "Heaven, yes. Finding the harmony, bringing the interior of the soul to a state of peace. That's the task, is it not? But to my mind the heart is the key, the gentle leader."

"Really? You sure about that? Let your heart lead? How's your back? Still sore, by the way you're carrying yourself."

John did not reply immediately. Then he admitted, "Well, yes it is."

"Aye. Then that's the catch in letting your heart rule over your head. It leads to trouble. Father John, you are the abbot; the eyes of your world are on you. Not much is hidden. Your love, your pain, your longings, what fires you. Your brothers see, and they follow. Even when they don't realize they see, they still follow when they don't understand. That's what being an abbot is all about. That's *why* you need a cool head."

John took this in.

"You have out-manoeuvred me," he said. "I think you always will. You are cleverer than I am. I respect your intelligence, and I am surely grateful for the help your head brings to this abbey. It's true I made a fool of myself, and I should have had the wit to see it coming. But even so, William – the bond between thee and me, the beautiful thread by which my finger-pads trace their way when I ask myself 'Is it well with his soul?' That thing – that's a matter of the heart."

Dust in the sunbeams. Quietness but for beasts shifting, blowing, chewing in their stalls below. The scent of hay. The sense of presence, of dear companionship. The present moment with its lode of life.

"It is, too," William said quietly. "And in my heart is where the other end of that thread is tied secure. I will never let it go. But look now, John, my head is insisting, you'd best be on your way. You'll be missed. If they find me here I haven't too many

170

other options. Let's keep it safe. And please – I beg you, please – don't say anything to Father Chad. It was childish of me to let something no more than obvious common sense smart so painfully. Don't raise it with him, I beg you. Just let it go."

"Huh!" John got up to leave.

"John – please!"

"Stay safe. I know you're stuck up here a long time each day, but don't pee on the hay if you can help it. I'll see you later."

"John –" But the abbot was descending the ladder, and checking that he was still unobserved as he left the stables.

He headed for the library. On the way, as he passed the guesthouse, the porter's lodge, the frater, first Brother Dominic, then Brother Martin, then Brother Richard, wanted to speak to him; but, "Not just now," he said.

He found Father Chad dusting books and tidying things away.

"Good morning, Brother," the abbot said pleasantly. "May I have a word?"

He related something of the hurt his probing in the hayloft had discovered, and asked his erstwhile prior to give account of himself.

Father Chad looked worried.

"I thought it for the best, Father John," he pleaded. "I know he likes to come here. I know he enjoys our company – but he had his chance at that, didn't he? And threw it away. He could have lived here every day of his life, but it wasn't enough. He had to be off on some other trail with an attractive scent. Now it seems that isn't enough either – he wants to be back here, finding out how things are going, stirring everything up. He can't seem to settle to anything; has to be peering over the fence. Can't seem to live with us in peace nor yet leave us in peace. No sooner he finds another place to be than he's back again, causing trouble. I'm sorry – honestly – if what I said upset him. But he put us in real danger yesterday."

John gazed, incredulous, at Father Chad.

"He's not... oh, you dimwit. You numbskull. You absolute *ninny*, Chad!" He knew he was sounding exactly like his sister Madeleine, but he didn't care. "It's not him causing trouble for us, you bird-brained bonehead; it's the other way round! There he was, peacefully at home out of harm's way, minding his own business and making his life work, until I went down there to beg him to come and help us – and right graciously he came, without one second's hesitation. He's stopped us spiralling down into chaos in the midst of this great nightmare influx of humanity; he's put himself between Cormac's impetuosity and the inevitable repercussions, and as a result of it his life is on the line – *again*. Causing trouble for us? Heaven bless us, man, can you not just *think* before you speak?"

Father Chad, mortified, blinked rapidly as he took this in. "I... I hadn't looked at it like that," he said. "You mean – you *asked* him to come back? And he a fugitive – an apostate?"

The abbot hesitated. Certainly, two legitimate courses of action had been open to him – expelling William or imprisoning him. Abetting his free choice to leave monastic profession to make a life with Madeleine was as grave a sin as William breaking his vows to go. He had brokered a spiritual adultery. Continuing any kind of friendship and interaction mired him, the abbot, in deeper. Severance and repentance were the only options allowed when a fully professed brother said he wanted to leave. John had chosen instead the complications of compromise. Every place the road forked along the way, the path he had taken seemed inevitable. But he could also see how the destination he'd reached would shock Father Chad. His vocation asked that he remain steadfast; instead he'd chosen to bend with the wind. He had followed his heart; the expression of bewilderment and distress on his librarian's face made him think that here was another man who thought he should have gone with his head.

This is what life and responsibility do to you, he thought; *this is the terrible power of human love. It dissolves all certainty. You make adjustments and modifications. Love and religion are uneasy bedfellows over time. It's hard to forget the screams of the man you burn at the stake. The act may have been accomplished in all righteousness, but you still lie awake at night, remembering the livid agony.* So here he stood, the guilty accomplice of kindness.

His brother in religion stood waiting. John had thought he came here to task Chad with his shortcomings; now it seemed the boot was on the other foot.

"Yes." The indignation left him, and his voice faltered as he answered. "Yes, I asked him to come back."

"And – is he still here?"

In a long, struggling silence, John looked at him. "Yes. Yes, he is… but – please –"

"Then, when you see him," said Father Chad, "will you tell him I am most heartily sorry. I hadn't understood."

Chapter
Six

There had been moments when John wondered if the bishop would ever go home. Ten days – *ten days*. He felt entirely certain the scrutiny of a monastery had never been so thorough or complete. No stone unturned. Dissected, visited and revisited and one more time for luck, the common life of St Alcuin's had been pinned back and laid bare. He did vaguely wonder if Brother Conradus's culinary acumen was partly responsible for this. But no matter; at long last his Lordship drew the abbey's visitation to a close, seeking one final audience with its shredded abbot.

"Your kitchens are marvellous," he pronounced; "your school is satisfactory; your guesthouse is pleasant and clean – not one insect bite have I suffered in the course of my stay. The daily round of life seems sober, orderly – even exemplary. Your stores are in good health, and your books well kept. Your novitiate is in good hands – *very* good hands. In general, I commend you. There is just one small thing, though. While your personal loyalty to your friends is no doubt admirable, I suspect it may be achieved at considerable cost to the faithful upholding of your obedience to the authority of Holy Church.

"I sat in your Chapter meeting – the day before yesterday, I believe – and the reading from the Rule reminded me again – now, what was it? Have you a copy handy? Thank you. Let me see... just a minute... Ah, yes – here we are. Regarding Sarabaites:

'Whatever enters their mind or appeals to them, that they call holy; what they dislike, they regard as unlawful.' It brought a little smile to my lips, Abbot John – because it reminded me of you."

His small, sharp, astute eyes rested meditatively on the abbot's face. "I am not easy to deceive," he said, "and I do believe you have tried to mislead and hoodwink me. I mean – let me make myself quite clear – with regard to your one-time brother of this house, William de Bulmer. Foxes are hard to surprise but easy to smell when they've been around. I don't know what game you are playing, Abbot John, but you can be sure of this: I will be watching. My reach is long. Word finds me. I have eyes in many places. And I do not like that man."

You and how many other people? thought John, but he lowered his eyes submissively, and did not speak.

"Well?" The bishop wanted a response.

Cautiously, John framed a reply. "I am sorry that your Lordship finds anything disappointing. I am sorry if something in my conduct is lacking, falls short of the mark. And I'm grateful and appreciative that you find so much to commend. All I can say of William de Bulmer is that our responsibility for him – our jurisdiction over him – ceased on the day he left us. Some of us were glad; he was not born to an easy life, and turbulence surely attends him. And yet, for all that, he loved and served us right well, in his way; he tried his best. He made mistakes in his life, as which of us do not? For the grief and trouble he caused, he was humbly sorry, and made the best reparation he could. Much like St Paul, Christ enlightened him, turned him around. The man you were seeking is already dead. His life is hid with Christ in God."

The bishop frowned. "William de Bulmer is dead? Well, why didn't you say so before, man? Are you making this up? You told me you knew nothing of his whereabouts!"

The abbot felt strongly tempted to roll with this misconstruction of what he had said, but felt it might lead to further trouble if he did. So he replied: "When a man leaves here, he is dead to us; and when a man is in Christ, he is a new creation."

The bishop contemplated him thoughtfully, then shook his head. "Be careful, Abbot John Hazell." The quiet menace of his voice was not lost on the abbot. Friendship with William turned out to be a hazardous undertaking indeed. And potentially costly.

But his Visitor picked up his gloves and made ready to be on his way. Not entirely easy in his mind, John watched him and his equerry ride out. He felt uncomfortably aware that, even with his best efforts, he could never guarantee to shelter either William or Madeleine from cruel and vindictive men bent on mischief; especially those whose arm came strengthened with the whole weight of the magisterium. It was not beyond possibility that he had jeopardized the peace and safety of every brother in his community; the men whose shepherd he was, the charge of their wellbeing placed in his trust. With a heavy heart he watched Brother Martin drop the great iron latch behind their departing inquisitor. This did not have the feel of a story entirely told.

Even so, he had other matters awaiting him. He walked back across the court to his lodging, sat at his table, picked up his pen, dipped it in the ink, and did what he might to train his thoughts into preparing a homily for Hannah's wedding.

"*Estote autem invicem benigni...*[5]" he wrote. He straightened his back, warily, wishing it didn't feel so sore it made him want to weep. He looked at the words he'd written and tried to think of something trenchant – or at the very least, coherent – to say about them. This would be his last chance to speak up for Hannah before the Bonvallet dynasty swallowed her up. Getting this right mattered.

5   "But ye be kind to one another" – a quotation from Ephesians 4:32

The latch to the cloister door rattled and lifted. John raised his head. It was his esquire. The abbot suppressed as best he could his frustration. Was it impossible for a man to find five uninterrupted minutes to work and think?

"I thought you and Stephen were going to get the rest of the bracken in," he said, trying hard to seem casually conversational.

"Aye – I was." Tom sounded as frayed as John felt. "I came back because I thought you might like to know, while you were with Bishop Eric this morning, Sir Geoffrey and Lady Agnes d'Ebassier arrived. Brother Dominic made them comfortable in the guesthouse, said you weren't free right then. But they're champing at the bit to come and greet you. They're wondering if they might not have to wait for suppertime, but can dine with you at midday as well. Being the case, it occurred to me you might be grateful for some back-up. So I searched out a lad from the novitiate to go up with Stephen. Brother Placidus. Cutting bracken isn't a complicated thing wanting expertise – I just like doing it. Oh, what? Not grateful?"

The abbot took this in. "I'm sorry, Tom," he said. "Of course I'm grateful. It's just… The d'Ebassiers… Whatever next? Oh, *Jesu, Maria*, oh heaven give me strength. Oh, my God. Oh, my Lord Jesus." He put down the quill and dropped his head into his hands.

"Hey – Father – John! I wasn't in earnest – about expecting you to be grateful, I mean; I was in earnest about the d'Ebassiers. It's all right. Look – I'll stall them. I'll send Francis over there to cheer 'em up. He can convey effusive greetings and salutations and tell 'em, yes, you'll be *delighted* to see them – at suppertime. How's that? You don't have to be at everyone's beck and call. And, when I've been to the guesthouse, will I nip up to the hayloft and give William the all-clear? Yes? And set our prisoner free?"

The abbot pulled himself together and looked his esquire in the eye, trying to summon a modicum of cheerfulness to meet his kindness. "Oh, glory – yes, please do," he said. "But, Tom! Caution William that the d'Ebassiers are here. Bishop Eric was not pleased about our concealment of William, nor fooled, by a long way. Best he avoids encounter with anybody he even *thinks* might know him."

"Aye, Father; consider it done. Back to your cogitations, then."

By the time Tom returned, he found his abbot had recovered his equilibrium.

"Tom," he said, "I'm embarrassed to be asking this, because I'm sure you'll already have told me and I've forgotten – have our cows calved well?"

"Aye, they have," said Tom, surprised that in the midst of all that had been going on, surrounded by guests and with final preparations for the wedding still requiring attention, John had time or inclination to think about the cows. "We had two bull calves and three heifers this spring – all fine, healthy animals."

"So, not counting the heifer calves, just the mothers, we have eight milk cows now?"

"Nine. When William was living with us, he extorted one in lieu of rent from some poor soul who'd fallen on hard times. After the summer rain, the man was all 'I'm so sorry, Father, I can't even afford to buy fodder for my cows'; to which William's reply was, 'Oh, really? Well, you can give one of them to us, then, and I'll write off a third of your debt.' Farmer looked fairly sour. He could see William had the better half of the bargain. But he didn't have much choice, so that's why we have nine cows."

"I see. Thank you." Tom waited, but the abbot said no more on the subject, and returned to the task of finishing off the homily for tomorrow, so his esquire got busy with his usual chores. As soon as John had roughed something out to his satisfaction, he left his atelier and went across to the checker, where he found Brother Cormac all the better for a few days' rest in a quiet cell.

On reflection, John thought he wouldn't have minded changing places.

"Can I have a look at our dairy yield records?" he asked the cellarer, and felt heartened to see Cormac could put his hand on them instantly and they were up to date and in immaculate order. He scanned the most recent page.

"But this... it's all in William's writing!"

Brother Cormac laughed. "Father John, you have no idea. He's been through these accounts like a gale force wind. He's been down here in the middle of the night with a candle, and here in the day when he knew the bishop was elsewhere. He's had every brother in the house on full alert as his watchdogs. Yes, our dairy record was a mish-mash of jottings, whatever Brother Stephen or I, or Tom passing through, thought to note down. Not good enough for William. He's been up at the farm asking questions, he copied out all the particulars and added in the new bits he'd gleaned from Stephen, wrote the whole thing out afresh in proper columns, and told me not to waste our old sheet but use it for kindling. And that was just the dairy yields!"

John said nothing to this, but looked carefully at the sums recorded. Eventually, "Seems to me we could manage with one less cow," he said.

✠   ✠   ✠

Surrounded by friends and family all jostling and straining to see, under a sky of brilliant blue adorned with scudding clouds of purest white, Hannah and Gervase exchanged their vows. Afterwards, as the cheerful, noisy throng of people poured into the church for Mass through the west door from the abbey court, William lingered outside. Though he'd promised to help serve food to the hordes of guests, he honestly wondered if this might be the moment to slip away. He detected and acknowledged the familiar bitter ache of exclusion, right down there deeper than his gut, than his bowel. In his core, the fountainhead of who he was. It hurt. John had once given him Eucharist in the privacy of the abbot's house, and had gone out on a limb for him, dared to break every rule for him. Compassionate. Forgiving. But having been a brother of this house, having broken his vows to Christ and walked away to marry Madeleine, there was no way back. The abbot could not possibly, in such a public setting, hold out the host of Christ's body for him to take. Though John had not formally excommunicated him, this far he could not go. And William knew it was his own doing, but it still felt like a deep, deep bruise.

He wanted to see the summer light slanting through the coloured glass of the lofty windows, and smell the incense. He wanted to hear the beautiful music Father Gilbert had prepared and made them practise every evening for the last heaven knows how many days. He wanted to hear the abbot's homily in this Mass. He wanted to be in the church, not just outside it; part of the holiness and the peace. Hungry, thirsty, tired; his soul. Without really consulting him, his feet trailed along with the rag-tag of the crowd, and he found a shadowed place to stand in the side aisle, leaning his shoulder against the curving body of one of the great sandstone pillars. And so the Mass began.

William listened to the familiar words of Christ's teaching, that before approaching the altar of God a man must be reconciled, must make peace where relationships are broken. He wondered if that was really the Gospel reading set for the day, or if this was Abbot John tweaking the rubric in a last desperate attempt to make the Bonvallets be nice to their unwelcome addition. He watched the abbot walk down to the chancel step to speak to the people. There he stood, dignified in the embroidered chasuble, bearing the weight on a slowly mending back, vested in the solemnity of his position. Abbot of this monastery, but the same man as the one who had stooped, knelt, in his simple black tunic, to wash and salve the burns and scrapes on William's body when he came here after the fire. The same man as had dissolved in convulsing agony of grief over the death of his mother, the angry pain of his sister. The same man who had come and found him in the hayloft and refused to budge until he heard the source of his misery. John. Healer. Friend.

The abbot murmured his dedication of the words he would speak, signing himself with the cross. He looked out across the people, then at the couple who stood together at the front.

"Hannah, Gervase, this Mass is celebrated in honour of your nuptials, and really these words are not for everyone else but for you.

"Not long ago, a friend commented to me that the idea of love baffled him at times. There were days when he felt an upwelling of affection towards his wife – delight in her – and others when, frankly, he wished she'd leave him in peace and he found her profoundly irritating. Here and there he came across fellow human beings whom he esteemed and with whom he felt a sense of fellowship, harmony. But not many. Mostly he preferred to go his own way and let everyone else go theirs. And guilt stirred in his soul, because he loved little, loved few – sometimes stopped loving even the one he had vowed and pledged to love, to have and to hold. And yet, he took seriously the command of Christ – to love and go on loving, to make that the mark of his discipleship and the work of his life.

"And my friend – humbly, neither cocksure nor evading the issue – put it to me that though he could not always find it within himself to love, he thought he could try to be kind. He said, in the course of his life he had been loved but rarely; and because of this, he valued with real gratitude those who had treated him with kindness. He said, sometimes he found it hard to tell whether someone actually loved him – cared for him with genuine

181

friendship – and when they were merely being kind to him. So, knowing himself to be a shrewd judge of men, he concluded love and kindness must be so extremely similar that the division between them is porous – where one ends and the other begins cannot readily be detected. He said this gave him hope, since, though love felt so often remote and mysterious, he knew how to be kind. Because, he said, everyone knows what kindness is. It means giving the other person the benefit of the doubt; including them, not cold-shouldering them; offering a smile and a cheerful greeting; making them a hot drink when they're tired and cold at the day's end; overlooking their shortcomings and their harmless – but intensely annoying – little mannerisms. It means giving them another chance. My friend also mentioned that it means trying not to swear at them too often, and forbearing from actually hitting them, however much you want to. He doesn't always find it easy to get on with his fellow man, or his wife – as you can tell.

"I thought – Gervase, Hannah – you might find it useful to hear about that conversation I had with my friend. Though today I hope you feel you are head over heels in love and will never be anything else, well, these vows are for a lifetime. I sincerely hope that means a substantial number of years for both of you. And maybe even today, you may be tired, you may feel somewhat strained; this is a big occasion, and family events always carry many resonances. Not all of them are easy.

"So I thought I'd put my companion's musings before you – that even when he runs out of love, forgets what love is, finds love impossibly difficult, he knows what kindness is; love's humble, less exalted, identical twin.

"God bless you in your life together. May you be happy, may you know bliss, may you be fruitful and content. And may you always at least try to be kind to one another – remembering that one of the most everyday habits of kindness is the willingness to try to understand, to forgive and begin again."

The abbot turned back into the sanctuary, and the Mass moved on through its rhythms of reconciliation and sanctification. There came the sharing of the peace – out of fashion but steadfastly maintained in the traditions of this house. "Peace be with you... peace be with you..." Those who stood close to William shook his hand in the *Pax Christi*, but their gaze didn't meet his. It was just a requirement, a formality. They didn't know him. They moved around, they moved on, shuffling and murmuring and turning from one to the other. He folded his arms across his belly, his back curving into a protective hunch that shut out the world as he took up his stance again, leaning against the sturdy York stone pillar, still slightly surprised to have encountered himself in a sermon, the echo of an evening conversation with John in the course of his stay.

Then, as the long thanksgiving and consecration prayers began, he became aware of a shifting in the people around him, making room for somebody coming to stand there, next to him. He turned his head, and to his astonishment saw Father Chad, who nodded at him in faintly embarrassed greeting, but did not speak, just stood beside him. They stood together, through the *Benedictus*, the epiclesis, the raising of the host, the singing of the beautiful, haunting, yearning *Agnus Dei*, the invitation of the people. As the great press of people moved forward to make their communion, William stood where he was; and Father Chad went on standing at his side.

Eventually, as those at the back began to make their way forward, the men were left behind in a space alone. In the privacy this created, Father Chad turned to William and said quietly, "The body of Christ." William looked at him. Then he understood. The teaching of Augustine that John, and Peregrine before him, brought again and again before the community had evidently sunk in. That the body of Christ, mystical, cosmic, immense, is in how we touch one another, how we are with each other, as well as in

183

the broken bread, blessed wine. It was very clear to Father Chad that William could not possibly participate in the sacrament. But there is more than one way to express the body of Christ.

From somewhere within and beneath him, arising from the earth under his feet, moving up through the whole of him, William felt a smile of purest peace and happiness; unexpected, startling. He whispered back the words he knew Chad meant to prompt – "I am." And Chad beheld what he would never have believed without seeing the evidence for himself: the shining of Christ's smile breaking through the fractured and shifting clouds of William's eyes.

The crowd formed around them again, returning. They stood there together through the final prayers, the benediction, watched the brothers process from the choir round into the south transept to the cloister door.

They still stood there as the multitude began to chatter and shift and find its way out into the sunshine in search of food and festivity. Eventually, once more they were alone.

"Thank you," said William.

"I'm sorry I didn't understand – before," said Chad. "About why you came here."

Silence fell between them, awkward and self-conscious, these men who essentially had nothing to say to each other and no time for each other, until now. Nothing but distrust on the one side and contempt on the other. Not fertile ground for friendship.

William took a deep breath, seeing some response must be necessary.

"It's only that…" he said, reluctant to bring out the truth of himself where he felt unsure it could be received, "only that… the first two decades of my life were a maelstrom of fear and loneliness… humiliation. The rest of it… I had to do as I might to piece the shards together into something that would hold up. But… well, the shards were me. There wasn't a wholeness to guide me, to show me how to go about it. No pattern to work from. I had to make it up as I went along, and all the time I still lived... like a wounded animal cornered, I guess. I'm sorry if this sounds intense and dramatic – I know that doesn't sit easy with you. But it's the only truth I have. It's what happened. You know what hell I ran from to come here. You know. It was my last hope. I... John touched me with kindness. He made a gap for me to crawl into. How could I forget that? How could I not come back? It was... like – no, it actually was – the open wound in Christ's side, to me. The way into his heart."

He made himself look, pleading, at Father Chad, and saw perplexity. "Then... why didn't you stay? If it meant so much to you."

"Because..." William sighed, looked away, moved restlessly. He hated this exposure of his roots. It was hard enough with John. With Father Chad it felt unbearable. But he could see that if he didn't take it now, this chance would never come again. "I came here to learn how to love, if that might be," he said. "I didn't know that, for me, 'love' and 'Madeleine' might as well be the same word, but that's how it turned out. I just *had* to, Chad – be with her, I mean. I had to go. All I can do is ask you to forgive me. I can't put it back now, even if I wanted to. Even if it doesn't make sense to you, can you not forgive me?"

Silence between them was measured then in heartbeats.

"And can *you* believe," said Chad then, "that you have been Christ's gift to me? I hated being the prior – it was too much for me. But I love working in the library, and in the garden. If it hadn't been for you, I'd probably have gone on being the blasted prior forever. I think I owe you a lot. But I'll be frank with you. This kind of thing isn't easy territory for me. The thunder and lightning that shakes and rattles around you just makes me want to stay inside with the door locked. I'm not that kind of man. I just like peace and quiet. I –"

But William cut him short, leaning towards him, the intensity that so disturbed Chad flaring in his burning, awful eyes. "*Yes!*" he said through clenched teeth. "For heaven's sake, brother! Can't you *see*? *So do I!*"

With more courage than he knew he possessed, Chad refrained from taking a step back, from dropping his gaze to escape the vehemence that beheld him.

"Then… why… why not just choose to live quietly?"

"Because, as you yourself pointed out to me, trouble follows me *every*where I go!"

This came cloaked in such expletives as Chad found shocking in this holy place.

"We are in church," he murmured reproachfully.

William stared at him. "'The body of Christ'," he said. "'I am.' Where are we not in church?"

A small involuntary sigh escaped Father Chad, and he sagged imperceptibly. "This was never going to be easy, was it?" he said. "Look, can we – will it be all right to settle simply for goodwill?"

William smiled. "I think we're past that. Heavens, man, you saved my life. You brought me Eucharist. I've passed through enough arid country, enough bleak desert where nothing grows, to treasure the flowers of kindness where I find them. I'm not about to forget. But I'd still be grateful to know myself forgiven."

Chad shook his head. "For what? By all holy, what a blessed tangle. This isn't simple, is it? There's no fault, no straightforward cause and effect. Too much of struggle and pain. The way you are, the way I am. What's to forgive? Let's just say we're friends, then – but, if it makes you feel better, for whatever you did – which escapes me now, we have too much history – for whatever the problem is; yes, most certainly I forgive you. And I hope that's mutual."

His eye caught by a movement, William looked across the nave to see Father Bernard come to check the church and see that everything was tidy.

"Time to go," he said quietly. He unfolded his arms. "Are we done?"

His cautious uncertainty made Father Chad smile. "Yes. Come on. I think Conradus could do with a hand serving all these people."

✠　　✠　　✠

As the day wore on, the wedding guests began to move and drift from their first situations. The close relatives of the Mitchell family, courteous and intelligent but supremely unsophisticated, sat with those of the Bonvallet clan and a handful of special guests – the d'Ebassiers notable among them – chosen to grace the occasion. But this was not a comfortable arrangement. Tired of smirks and raised eyebrows, in search of a good time, one by one the Mitchells found excuse to wander outside, find the man with the hurdy-gurdy and watch the jugglers. Eventually Hannah whispered to Gervase and he smiled, took her hand, explained to his mother that he had a duty to greet his guests outside; and the bride and groom went, too.

For a while, Abbot John sat in the place graciously allocated to him, then as the set piece began to break up, he too felt it right to wander among the guests of his house, and extend a welcome beyond the aristocracy.

He found his way to the tables serving food and ale (the fine wines were reserved for those deemed worthy to sit down with the mice in the refectory), where William had been helping Rose and Gavin and Brother Conradus, serving the milling crowd of guests.

There Abbot John made a point of talking with Brother Conradus's father Gavin, expressing his appreciation of Conradus's work in the kitchen and his hearty thanks for sparing Rose from her duties at home to help them with the wedding preparations. Rose smiled at his honest gratitude, which he was careful to couch in terms that made much of her role in life as Gavin's wife.

Then he stood at William's side for a while, watching the groups of guests filling the whole of the abbey court.

"A bit of an eye-opener – some of these new styles of dress," observed the abbot, watching a knot of young men and women talking and laughing together. The girls' sideless surcoats ("gates of hell", John had heard them called), the shorter and shorter tunics of the men, these had all been designed and cut not to cover but to titillate and reveal. "What d'you think of them, William?"

His friend looked up from the pastries he'd been organizing onto one serving dish to free up space so he could stack platters to go back to the kitchen.

"Of what? The lads or the lasses? Oh, both? Depends who's wearing what. I noticed Lady Florence has ventured into one of these gates of hell, but by St Peter, any man who reached his hand in there for a quick squeeze would more likely be turned to stone than find himself all aflame. And those parti-coloured hose and stupid little tunics? Don't leave much to the imagination, do they? I'd rather keep my crown jewels a bit better protected than that! Still, you know what, Abbot John? It's well to remember, you and I are growing into old men. 'Tis the shortest possible step from here to Lady Gunhilde's observation tower: 'We'd never have worn anything like that in *my* day. *We* were brought up properly. We *knew* how to dress with dignity.' A top-up of ale, my lord?" (This last addressed not to John but to a young man unaccountably still thirsty.) "Here you are." John watched him pour, precisely, never a drip, set the flagon down with care, well away from the edge of the table. Though William had schemed and worked his way to the highest possible status in monastic life, his childhood as general dogsbody trained by exacting standards and unremitting cruelty, had certainly left him able to serve ale without spilling a single drop and wait very effectively upon these guests.

"But, nay – modesty and sobriety are in equally short supply here. Wearing their wares, as you might say. Personally, I find reticence and decency a lot more attractive. And I've noticed you do, too."

Seeing the discomfiture in the abbot's face, he apologized quickly. "I'm only teasing you," he said. "I think. But now then, Abbot John, apparel doesn't make the man, nor yet the woman. It's what they say, it's the look in their eye – are they merciful, are they gentle, are they respectful, are they kind? That's what to look for, and who cares what they wear? Talk to 'em."

The abbot took this gentle hint, and in the course of the afternoon he made sure to give all the gracious attention of a good host to the assorted members of the Bonvallet and Mitchell tribes, as well as to Sir Geoffrey and Lady Agnes d'Ebassier and all the guests of substance, but also to the lesser folk congregated out in the sunshine, and to the minstrels and friends from the village who had come to help and serve. He listened, he smiled, he complimented, laughed in the right places; and when the bell rang for None he decided he'd done enough.

Walking across the abbey court towards the church's western door, he paused once more by the serving tables. "When Conradus comes back from chapel, can you take a moment to find me in my house?" he asked his friend. "Am I right in thinking you'll be wanting to be on your way home tomorrow morning?"

William nodded. "I'd thought of going home at the end of the afternoon when the guests begin to leave," he said, "but it looks as though you could do with a hand clearing up at the end, so I'll stay. Tomorrow, as you say. And, yes, I'll drop by in a little while when you've done praying."

"He's been a Godsend," said Gavin with a grin, leaning forward to speak past William to the abbot. "You couldn't call him stingy with the ale, but he knows when to stop pouring! Makes it go round. And he can get a dozen slices out of a pie our Rose meant for ten."

Brother Conradus wiped his hands on a cloth, shook it out, folded it neatly and set it down handy for future use, then came round the table to walk with his abbot to chapel.

"I bet I can guess who that friend of yours is – the one who finds love such a puzzle and a struggle," he said.

His abbot smiled. "Yes. I think you probably can. I liked his solution, though."

"Aye, indeed. I do, too. Well, I do believe it's been a success, Father John. All that hard work has been well worthwhile. I hope Sir Cecil is pleased with everything. William says the man is generous in his donations to us. He thinks we may be out of pocket over the wedding, but it'll pay off in the end. I hadn't really thought of it in those terms, but I see what he means. William's a shrewd man – good to have him on our side."

"Oh yes," agreed his abbot, as they came through the open doors of the rood screen into the choir. "That's a fact!"

Avoiding the abbey court when the afternoon office concluded, in the silence of the cloister John trod slowly along to his house. He could feel the beginnings of normality re-settling like dust after a gust of wind subsides. The hubbub of music, talk and laughter still seeped through from the refectory and wafted up from the court beyond the west range, blowing around the precincts. But here, with the cool green of the cloister garth shining through the arches, in the lights and shadows of the stone walkway, he felt the ancient current of serenity, an unbroken thread of peace weaving through to the surface again. In all honesty, he couldn't quite feel his way back to it; a tangle of uncomfortable longings still conflicted his heart. He could not claim to have reached equilibrium; but he could sense the healing peace of the house re-establishing, and for that he was grateful.

He sat in the quiet of his lodge, for once undisturbed by people wanting him. Today saw them all fully engaged with the duties of hospitality. He was surprised that when he heard the awaited familiar knock, it was neither on the door to the outer court, nor the inner door to the cloister, but the small door by the scribe's desk, the little escape to the path under the birch trees, leading to the river.

"You seem well acquainted with this little door," he commented, as he opened it to admit his friend. "Most people don't even notice it."

William grinned. "I realize that. 'Tis why it's there. I had one too, at St Dunstan's, and it saved my skin. Every life needs an unobtrusive exit. I didn't want folk to see me come to your lodging – didn't want to give them the notion you might be at home and receiving visitors."

John smiled. "You understand so well. Anyhow, sit you down; that's right. There's a small thing I need to sort out before you pack up to go. Would you like a cow?"

Taken aback by this completely unexpected question, William laughed. "A cow? Aye, I surely would. But what – why – ?"

"A gift from us here, to thank you – and Madeleine, coping at home without you – for all your help and hard work in these last few days. I was thinking if we had anything that might please you, and unless I'm mistaken you still have no cow, only a goat. We can spare a young one – she calved earlier in the spring. Her calf's weaned off onto the bucket now. So she should milk through, you won't have to take her to the bull for a good long while. She's fit and healthy, last you a good few years. Would that be welcome?"

"Oh, aye, it would indeed! Madeleine *might* be pleased to see me – I mean I hope she will, even with a fading black eye; but that she'll be overjoyed to see a cow I am entirely certain. God bless you, John; that would make a lot of difference to us. Are you sure you can spare her?"

"I'm not sure I need to answer that. I looked over the milk yields this morning, and whose hand did I read, neat and meticulous, missing nothing? You know exactly what we have, in every chest and storeroom, every barn and orchard, every sty and byre: of that I'm sure. Of course we can spare her. Tom can go up and milk her in the morning and bring her down to the gate. You don't mind walking a cow ten miles home?"

William smiled. "You might be wise not to tell her that's how far she has to walk; but no, that'll be fine. We can start out early and take it slow. Thank you. That's a handsome gift indeed. And unexpected."

✠   ✠   ✠

Monks get up early.

William stole silently out of the guesthouse as the flush of dawn began to give way to blue, not wishing to disturb the slumbering guests as he stepped with care over close-packed bodies. He very much hoped to find the abbot waiting for him as he trod purposeful and light to the gatehouse. He really wanted the cow, but it felt imperative to delay his return no longer. And there stood his brother-in-law, the end of a long, stout tether loosely held in one hand. The other end attached to a rope halter about the head of a milk cow the colour of a lightly cooked loaf of white wheat flour. She was cropping the grass where it grew long and lush in the place trees grew adjacent to the court. She swung up her head, chewing, and regarded William's approach with placid, enormous eyes of darkest brown. He liked her.

"I can well imagine you want urgently to be home," John said, in an undertone appropriate to the time of day. "But let me walk along the road with you a little way."

Beyond an initial smile of welcome, William said nothing. The abbey was still wrapped in the Grand Silence, its guests fast asleep in the house beside them, windows open through the summer night. Talking could wait until they were beyond its gates. The porter was not yet at his post. William hitched his pack firmly onto his back and took the rope from the abbot's hand. With as little noise as he could manage, John drew back the bolt on the postern door in the big gate, surprising William by latching it behind them after they passed through. He said nothing, waiting for John to speak, as they ambled along at the peaceful pace of a cow.

"I have four things to say to you," John began after they had walked the whole length of the abbey approach and came onto the open road. His friend alongside him, easy and quiet, waited to hear what they would be.

"The first thing I think I have never put into words is that I love you for many reasons, but not least for the quality of your silence. I have never felt less judged by anyone. You have the knack of giving a man room, freedom to breathe. I would say it is kindness, but that doesn't feel right. It's more spacious than that. You simply leave me alone, leave me in peace; and yet, there you are. It's more comforting than I know how to tell you. You see?" He grinned at William, teasing. "You don't even say 'Thank you.' Just silence, accepting. I can feel it like a shawl around me, light and warm. For that – and for other things, but that will do for today, I don't want you to get too big-headed – I love you.

"Then, the second thing... is... I'm sorry. Sorry that I let myself fall into that trap like a silly boy. Not that she set a snare for me – by no means. I should have known better, and I should be setting you a faithful example, not relying on you to keep me to the path. I am so sorry."

They paused awhile for their companion to sample the herbage growing leafy and tender from the rain-ditch, as they turned off the road that continued to the village, taking the lane branching west through farmland, the way home for William now. Still William did not speak. *Then how does his sympathy touch me?* John wondered. *How do I feel his understanding so unmistakably clear?*

"The third thing – I beg you, William – please forgive me. I put you in such jeopardy. They would have had you on a gibbet without a second thought. I put your life at risk. I don't know what I can have been thinking, to ask you to come and help while the bishop was with us. Well – I do know really; I was thinking about myself and my own problems. But I never anticipated I'd land you in such trouble. And I haven't forgotten you telling me the basis of good leadership is anticipation. I guess that makes me a rotten abbot. I nearly cost you your life. Please forgive me.

"And then –"

Now William interrupted him. "Look, does this list of your sins and my virtues get much longer? It's a novelty for me, and I'm enjoying it, but we live only ten miles away. We might get there before you've finished, even at this speed. Can I just say, you are welcome to eat with us if we reach Caldbeck before you stop talking."

John grinned. "I thank you. But I have only one more item on my list. I am so grateful for everything you've done for us; so very grateful. You know. You know quite well how much we needed your help and what a difference it made. I want to make sure you also know how deeply appreciated it is. William –" He stopped and waited until William would lift his gaze, embarrassed by such praise, to meet John's eyes. "*Thank you.*"

"You are most welcome"; William made no attempt at a jest. "If I've been in any way of service to you, it makes me happy. Now, have you done? Do I get a turn?"

He stood still, looking down at the ground, the thumb of his left hand thrust in his belt, his right hand holding the tether. John waited, intrigued. "Yes?"

"Only this." He did not look up. "My brother, give yourself time to grieve. You stepped back from a most magnificent blunder in these last few days; and you were right to do so. Nothing holy or strong could possibly have come from it – only either embarrassment or misery. But no one knows better than I do how hard it is to make such a renunciation. Being right is precious little consolation. When you came into religious life as a young man, I suppose you were full of fire and vision, all ready to follow Christ unto the end. Were you?" He glanced up at him then.

John nodded. "Something like that."

"And then in mid-life, there comes this awful craving for comfort, for gentleness, for somebody to touch you tenderly, for peaceful companionship. A longing to be held. But this time there's no spark left to kindle the fire of vocation, and no real vision – just a life. Nothing more inspiring than a deep sense of responsibility and the knowledge that other people depend on you. Which is not a little thing, but it doesn't taste of glory. What it comes down to is that – and this is a bit rich coming from me, don't I know it – even so – just that I'm so proud of you, John. And that I know it leaves you limping. Be kind to yourself as much as you would to anyone else. Seriously. Give yourself time to grieve. And leave that abominable, loathsome scourge of yours lie where I flang it in the river." He took a deep breath. "Right then, old friend. Home waits. Better be on our way."

And so they parted. The abbot stood for a moment watching him stroll away; by no means in a straight line but according to the whim of his companion as the attractions of greenstuff at this side and that drew her fancy. John smiled at the sight, then turned to walk back along the rutted lanes to the abbey green and the stone-flagged open ground before St Alcuin's imposing doors set into the huge arch of the gateway.

He thought about William's words, and about the way he had come – his long journey from insouciant boyhood to heavy responsibilities of the abbacy. He thought about the meaning of his vocation, the daily round of this life; and now he dared to think about Rose – that brief, bright, impractical interlude. And yes, he knew it was in the past; and yes, as William saw, that brought grief. A stinging, painful fissure in his soul.

Glad it was still too early for anyone except the community to be stirring, he walked across the court to the church, in through the west door standing open for any who wished to attend the morrow Mass, along the side-aisle to the spacious, empty nave, into the choir. He genuflected before the presence of Christ in the blessed sacrament, and turned aside to the by now familiar sanctum of the abbot's stall. He pulled his cowl up over his head and closed his eyes. In the silence he sat, quiet and simple, unmoving, allowing that grief to be – the grief of human loneliness in the uncertainty and vulnerability of life; the grief of choosing celibacy, even with all the richness of its gift and possibility; the grief of renouncing, of not clinging, of giving back, surrendering, asking nothing. But he caught the moment when grief slid almost imperceptibly into self-pity, and opened his eyes again. He watched his brothers, their different shapes and sizes, variety of gait, their serious, recollected faces, their disciplined quietness. He thought maybe he had held their trust in him too light. In the innermost intimate place of his heart, silently he touched the presence of the living Christ, and asked forgiveness; not for loving, but for forgetting that he also loved these men, and was called to serve them.

Then the time came for him to don chasuble and stole, to take up the consecrated duties of his office, step out of the simple human struggle of his heart into the holy vocation of the priesthood. He celebrated the Mass, holding high the broken earthly body of the bread for the Holy Spirit to come in and bring the mystery of Jesus. He stooped to his kneeling brothers – "the body of Christ... the body of Christ..." – knowing they had seen his weakness, his stumbling, the longing he could not cover up, but still had the humility to kneel and take the bread of heaven from his fallible, human hands. And these same hands, with their broken lifelines of compromise and sadness, spread in blessing over his brothers and sent them into Chapter – where he was more glad than he could say to have neither Brainard nor Bishop Eric in evaluative attendance, watching and waiting for heresy and error.

Today, Father Gilbert read the chapter from the Rule; then John addressed them.

"My brothers, there's something I wanted to say to you – just for the community, not to put before a wider audience. Because it's an idea half-formed and possibly heretical; so I rely on you to forgive me if I've got it wrong.

"Our lives in religion are governed and directed by the teachings of Holy Church. We study the writings of the Desert Fathers and the holy apostles. We learn and recite the creeds. We reverence the dogma of the church with all solemnity. And in our creeds and our dogma, we learn about the lordship of Christ, how the Holy Spirit proceeds towards us, how Christ died and harrowed hell and rose again, then ascended into heaven. We learn that the Father, Son and Holy Spirit are the three in one – indivisible, three perspectives upon one God. We learn that our salvation relies upon submitting to faith in Christ – surrendering our will and our intellect to the doctrines of the church. We learn that the church militant here on earth is Christ's body, conjoined in eternal life with the great communion of saints and martyrs.

"This is our faith – the faith of the church. It straightens out for us who Jesus is – our Lord and Master – and what we must believe about him, as Christian people.

"*But*. Oh dear, why is there always a 'but'? The thing is, in living by the creeds and doctrines of Holy Church, precious though they undoubtedly are, in giving our lives to the study and propagation of religious dogma, we can very readily become inflexible. We can easily allow ourselves to become harsh and inquisitorial, focused on being right, demanding that the thoughts and behaviour of our brothers meet our – occasionally impossible – standards.

"When we say 'Jesus is Lord', it's a confession of faith and a pledging of allegiance; but we ought also to pause and consider *who Jesus is*.

"Jesus was the one who said that by this would all men know that we are his disciples – that we love one another. Jesus held out to Judas the sop of bread dipped in wine, reserved for the honoured guest. Jesus, risen, asked Peter three times, 'Do you love me?' Peter, who denied him three times. Jesus came between the righteousness of the mob gathered with stones in their hands, and the woman taken in adultery. Jesus, called as the messiah of the children of Israel, nevertheless stopped and answered the pleas of the Gentile woman whose daughter was demonized. She had no other recourse, and he stopped, he heard her prayer.

"This is our Lord. He was honest – excoriatingly so at times, when he saw pride and arrogance, contempt and indifference. He lived in devastating simplicity, owning (so far as we know) nothing, settling nowhere. 'The Son of Man has nowhere to lay his head.'

"Such simplicity bestows, on the pilgrim who lives it, spaciousness. He was not preoccupied, as we are, with masonry and keeping butter cool and the price of grain. He made himself wholly available as an open channel for the generosity of God. He depended on the kindness of others to live entirely for kindness himself. For love. For grace.

"I want to put it to you, my brothers, that though we do indeed hold in reverence the teaching of Holy Church, submitting ourselves to it in holy obedience, even so the church is not our Lord. Jesus is. Dogma and credos are not our master. Jesus is.

"His is the way in which we are pledged to walk, his the

discipline that must form our habits of life and mind. And that is both infinitely easier and infinitely harder than losing ourselves in the hair-splitting delights of theological intricacy. Jesus asks of us – shows us – simplicity, and kindness. That's it. That's what it boils down to. That's what he wants of us. To make the best we can of every day. To find the way the light shines on. To serve the cause of kindness. And, so far as it lies with us, to do the little, cheerful things that make people happy.

"If that sounds small to you – not amounting to very much – well, try it. You just try it. I'll have to ask Father Theodore later if I'm wide of the mark. But it's what feels true to me, anyhow."

✠   ✠   ✠

As the days had gone by, Madeleine had passed through patience (swiftly) to impatience, to indignation, to outrage.

At first, though she felt vulnerable at home without William, and the evenings were lonely, she told herself to be proud and pleased that they could help the community at St Alcuin's in this way – her brother's community, who had been so good to her and to William, sheltering each of them in their time of need. It repaid a debt and restored a relationship for William to spend this time with them, assisting Brother Cormac, offering the support and guidance of his shrewd mind and years of experience.

The nights were chilly, but hardly cold enough for the indulgence of a fire. She knew William would never reproach her for using firewood unnecessarily; but without question he'd notice. Without the cheerful comfort of the fire, the hours seemed mournfully long. She made her fire of sticks in the bread oven, of course, for her daily loaf, and a small fire on the hearth for her porridge in the morning. Then she ate bread with butter and cheese made from Marigold's milk, accompanied by salad greens from the hedgerow and the garden. She didn't eat the eggs, saving them to sell in the market when William came home: somehow she didn't want to go without him – not into the town among all the people on market day. She felt safer with him at her side. She examined this thought, asking herself what exactly she feared. She found no answer. She had to acknowledge that he completed her, somehow; she felt a little lost, as though her strength ebbed, away from his side. This surprised her; she had never imagined herself as one to lean on someone else. She wondered if he felt the same.

The quiet, steady ache of loneliness gave way to puzzlement as the passing days increased. John had said the bishop's Visitation would be three days only, and by the end of that time William should have set Cormac up with all the advice he needed to fulfil the extra hospitality occasioned by the wedding. She wondered if something had gone wrong.

As day gave way to day, the solitude got to her. She missed William, she couldn't think what could be keeping him so long, and the thought drifted into her mind – and stuck – that all men are outrageously selfish. Cormac needed help – very well, so did she. John could do with William at his side – what about her? Women, she thought, were there to pick up and put down; to turn to when nothing more interesting came along to claim the attention of their menfolk. Men prioritized their own pursuits above the needs of their wives. Men walked down the middle of the road, leaving the womenfolk to pick their way along the ditch edge.

By the time he'd been away a week, Madeleine began to think if she could get on without him this long, William might as well stay away forever. She felt hurt and neglected, affronted at this level of abandonment. After ten days she decided she never wanted to see him again.

Then a cold fear settled into her heart. What if he'd been set on by robbers on the way home? What if the bishop had taken

200

exception to him, had him clapped in irons and hauled him off to be tried for heresy or apostasy in the ecclesiastical court? Given William's life-long record of upsetting almost everyone he met, this seemed not unlikely. What if he never came home? What if this was it now – just her alone in this spacious, beautiful house, with the goat and the chickens but the light of no human soul to keep her company? Angry, frightened and cold in bed at night, she began to panic.

Had he left her? Had he decided married life suited him no better than his monastic vows after all, and simply walked away? Had he caught the plague and died? Had they all, that they sent no word?

She felt as though her being grew smaller, shrivelling into endurance, scared and upset. She knew the day of the wedding, and thought it would be in the morning, so perhaps he'd return in the evening of that day. So through the afternoon she worked outside, listening, always listening. But still William didn't come home. The next day, she thought he must surely come, and at every smallest sound she lifted her head alert. As the sun sank and its rays lengthened across the orchard and she took the pail out to milk Marigold as evening came, she began to despair.

And then she heard the familiar, unmistakable clack of the iron latch to their yard gate. She stripped off the udder with all speed, followed with a cursory wipe down, moved the pail out of kicking range, and flew off to investigate, leaving Marigold still tied up, bleating indignantly once her knot of dried herbs was all gone.

"What in the *world*?"

Madeleine stopped dead, taking in at one and the same time the green and yellow bruising of her husband's black eye, and the honey-coloured cow traipsing alongside him, led by a rope and a halter, her swinging swollen udder dripping with milk.

"Let me deal with that. William, where in heaven have you been? Where did you get this cow? There's fresh bread in the kitchen. Why have you got a black eye, for heaven's sake? Whatever have you been doing? What can possibly have kept you so long? Oh, heaven, I've been so worried! Did she follow you all the way home, on the halter like that? Has she had a drink? Here, let me, poor thing; look! Her udder's that tight!"

He resisted her attempts to take the cow from him, putting the hand that held the rope behind his back. He reached out his other hand, caught his wife to him and kissed her. Then, "I am so sorry," he said. "You must have been out of your mind with worry. Your brother gave us this cow to thank us – both of us – for putting ourselves out like this to help him. The black eye – it's a long story; almost as long as the way home has been. I set out bright and early but Honey has stopped at every clump of fresh green grass and likely looking patch of sprouting worts. She's tired, I'm tired, I'm almighty glad to see you, and I'll be glad of the bread and grateful to you for seeing to milking her. I've never milked a cow. John tells me it's not the same as a goat – you'll have to show me."

When she came in half an hour later, with a brimming pail of cow's milk in one hand and a smaller can of goat's milk in the other, excited at the possibilities for cheese and butter, Madeleine found her husband sitting at the table, breadcrumbs, cheese rinds and an empty ale mug telling a tale of supper completed. He held a rosary in his hands.

"Heaven bless us, this is new!" she said. "You *have* come home devout!"

"It's John's."

She could tell from the quality of his quietness that a great deal had happened. She knew she'd hear all about it as they lay curled up in bed together under the sturdy rafters of their home.

"He asked me if I had a rosary," said her husband, "and I said no. Well – there's yours, but I no longer have one of my own. So he took his off and gave it to me, asking me to pray for him;

that Our Lady's faithfulness to the call of God on her life would pass into his heart forever. That the steadfast perseverance of the Lord Jesus would keep his feet in the path of salvation. That the practical soul of St Benedict would keep watch over him. That his fingers would find the thread of life and loving kindness, and never let go. So that's what I was doing."

The story of the monks of
St Alcuin's continues in

A Day and a Life

(coming June 2016)

Glossary and Explanatory Notes

The recipe for goose roast alive is an actual recipe, from the sixteenth-century *Magia Naturalis*. So the recipe itself is later than the setting of this book, but gives a sense of the scope of grisly invention in medieval cookery. My source can be found online here: www.godecookery.com/incrd/incrd.htm#009

Hebdomedarian – The reader for the day/week

"*Taille haut*" – Thirteenth-century precursor of the eighteenth-century hunting cry "Tally-ho!" Meaning, in effect, "swords at the ready", as a quarry comes into view.

"*Un ange passe*" – Literally, "an angel is passing"; a French expression accounting for the sudden silences that sometimes occur in a social setting.

Wes hal – Old English traditional greeting (the word "wassail" comes from this, and "hello" or "hallo"); literally means "be thou whole".

The French jokes in Chapter Two
These are all well-worn puns. In religious life, a priest is "Father" (Fr.: Père); an abbess is "Mother" (Fr.: Mère); a nun is "Sister" (Fr.: Soeur). The abbot is l'Abbé.

The puns are all aural plays, making common French words sound like the names of monastics, as follows:

l'Abbé Bé – "la bébé" = the baby. "Puéril" = "childish"

Père Plexe – "pèreplexe" = perplexed. "Religieux, mais dubitative" = "Religious, but doubtful."

Père Missif – Brainard says, "Eh bien, peut-être ça c'est le Père Missif" – means, "Well, then, perhaps it's Père Missif". A pun on "pèrmissif" = permissive.

"Un peu trop laxiste," replies the bishop – which means, "A little too lax."

Mère Itante – "Ou bien, la Mère Itante," says Hubert. "Ou bien" means "or". Mère Itante is a pun on "mèritante", meaning "deserving". Percival replies: "Qui a bien gagnée sa place au ciel!" This means, "Who has certainly won her place in heaven!"

L'Abbé Casse – A pun on "la bécasse" = "woodcock". "Un drôle d'oiseau!" = "A comical sort of bird".

Soeur Titude – A pun on "certitude" – the English word being the same. Certainty. "Enfin" means "then" in this context, or "after all". The reply is, "Mais on n'a jamais été sûr d'elle" – meaning, "but you can never rely on her".

L'Abbé Névole – A "bénévole" is a volunteer. The reply, "Oui – car celui-çi ne demande jamais rien", means, "Yes, because he never asks for anything."

L'Abbé Nédiction – A pun on "benediction" = a blessing or grace.

Monastic Day

There may be slight variation from place to place and at different times from the Dark Ages through the Middle Ages and onward – e.g., Vespers may be after supper rather than before. This gives a rough outline. Slight liberties are taken in my novels to allow human interactions to play out.

Winter Schedule (from Michaelmas)
2:30 a.m. Preparation for the nocturns of matins – psalms, etc.
3:00 a.m. Matins, with prayers for the royal family and for the dead.
5:00 a.m. Reading in preparation for Lauds.
6:00 a.m. Lauds at daybreak and Prime; wash and break fast (just bread and water, standing).
8:30 a.m. Terce, Morrow Mass, Chapter.
12:00 noon Sext, Sung Mass, midday meal.
2:00 p.m. None.
4:15 p.m. Vespers, Supper, Collatio.
6:15 p.m. Compline.
The Grand Silence begins.

Summer Schedule
1:30 a.m. Preparation for the nocturns of matins – psalms etc.
2:00 a.m. Matins.
3:30 a.m. Lauds at daybreak, wash and break fast.
6:00 a.m. Prime, Morrow Mass, Chapter.
8:00 a.m. Terce, Sung Mass.
11:30 a.m. Sext, midday meal.
2:30 p.m. None.
5:30 p.m. Vespers, Supper, Collatio.
8:00 p.m. Compline.
The Grand Silence begins.

Liturgical Calendar

I have included the main feasts and fasts in the cycle of the church's year, plus one or two other dates that are mentioned (e.g., Michaelmas and Lady Day when rents were traditionally collected) in these stories.

Advent – begins four Sundays before Christmas.

Christmas – December 25th.

Holy Innocents – December 28th.

Epiphany – January 6th.

Baptism of our Lord concludes Christmastide, Sunday after January 6th.

Candlemas – February 2nd (Purification of Blessed Virgin Mary, Presentation of Christ in the temple).

Lent – Ash Wednesday to Holy Thursday – start date varies with phases of the moon.

Holy Week – last week of Lent and the Easter Triduum.

Easter Triduum (three days) of Good Friday, Holy Saturday, Easter Sunday.

Lady Day – March 25th – this was New Year's Day between 1155 and 1752.

Ascension – forty days after Easter.

Whitsun (Pentecost) – fifty days after Easter.

Trinity Sunday – Sunday after Pentecost.

Corpus Christi – Thursday after Trinity Sunday.

Sacred Heart of Jesus – Friday of the following week.

Feast of John the Baptist – June 24th.

Lammas (literally "loaf-mass"; grain harvest) – August 1st.

Michaelmas – feast of St Michael and All Angels, September 29th.

All Saints – November 1st.

All Souls – November 2nd.

Martinmas – November 11th.